# The Hardy Boys
# Casefiles™

# Franklin W. Dixon

# The Hardy Boys Casefiles™

## Dead on Target

## Evil, Incorporated

Armada
*An Imprint of* HarperCollins*Publishers*

*Dead on Target* and *Evil, Incorporated*
were first published in the USA in 1987 by
Simon & Schuster, Inc.
First published in Great Britain in Armada in 1989

First published together in this edition
in 1993 by Armada
Armada is an imprint of
HarperCollins Children's Books,
part of HarperCollins Publishers Ltd
77-85 Fulham Palace Road
Hammersmith, London W6 8JB

1 3 5 7 9 10 8 6 4 2

Printed and bound in Great Britain by
HarperCollins Book Manufacturing, Glasgow

# Chapter

## 1

"GET OUT OF my way, Frank!" Joe Hardy shoved past his brother, shouting to be heard over the roar of the flames. Straight ahead, a huge fireball rose like a mushroom cloud over the parking lot. Flames shot fifty feet into the air, dropping chunks of wreckage—wreckage that just a moment earlier had been their yellow sedan. "Iola's in there! We've got to get her out!"

Frank stared, his lean face frozen in shock, as his younger brother ran straight for the billowing flames. Then he raced after Joe, catching him in a flying tackle twenty feet away from the blaze. Even at that distance they could feel the heat.

"Do you want to get yourself killed?" Frank yelled, rising to his knees.

Joe remained silent, his blue eyes staring at the wall of flame, his blond hair mussed by the fall.

Frank hauled his brother around, making Joe face him. "She wouldn't have lasted a second," he said, trying to soften the blow. "Face it, Joe."

For an instant, Frank thought the message had gotten through. Joe sagged against the concrete. Then he surged up again, eyes wild. "No! I can save her! Let go!"

Before Joe could get to his feet, Frank tackled him again, sending both of them tumbling along the ground. Joe began struggling, thrashing against his brother's grip. With near-maniacal strength, he broke Frank's hold, then started throwing wild punches at his brother, almost as if he were grateful to have a physical enemy to attack.

Frank blocked the flailing blows, lunging forward to grab Joe again. But a fist pounded through his guard, catching him full in the mouth. Frank flopped on his back, stunned, as his brother lurched to his feet and staggered toward the inferno.

Painfully pulling himself up, Frank wiped something wet from his lips—blood. He sprinted after Joe, blindly snatching at his T-shirt. The fabric tore loose in his hand.

Forcing himself farther into the glare and suffocating heat, Frank managed to get a grip on his brother's arm. Joe didn't even try to shake free. He just pulled both of them closer to the flames.

The air was so hot it scorched Frank's throat as he gasped for breath. He flipped Joe free, throwing him off balance. Then he wrapped one arm around Joe's neck and cocked the other back, flashing in a karate blow. Joe went limp in his brother's arms.

As Frank dragged them both out of danger, he heard the wail of sirens in the distance. We should never have come, he thought, never.

Just an hour before, Joe had jammed the brakes on the car, stopping in front of the mall. "So *this* is why we had to come here," he exclaimed. "They're having a rally! Give me a break, Iola."

"You knew we were working on the campaign." Iola grinned, looking like a little dark-haired pixie. "Would you have come if we'd told you?"

"No way! What do you think, we're going to stand around handing out Walker for President buttons?" Joe scowled at his girlfriend.

"Actually, they're leaflets," Callie Shaw said from the backseat. She leaned forward to peer at herself in the rearview mirror and ran her fingers hastily through her short brown hair.

"So that's what you've got stuck between us!" Frank rapped the cardboard box on the seat.

"I thought you liked Walker," said Callie.

"He's all right," Frank admitted. "He looked good on TV last night, saying we should fight back against terrorists. At least he's not a wimp."

"That antiterrorism thing has gotten a lot of coverage," Iola said. "Besides . . ."

3

". . . He's cute," Frank cut in, mimicking Iola. "The most gorgeous politician I've ever seen."

Laughter cleared the air as they pulled into a parking space. "Look, we're not really into passing out pamphlets—or leaflets, or whatever they are," Frank said. "But we will do something to help. We'll beef up your crowd."

"Yeah," Joe grumbled. "It sounds like a real hot afternoon."

The mall was a favorite hangout for Bayport kids—three floors with more than a hundred stores arranged around a huge central well. The Saturday sunshine streamed down from the glass roof to ground level—the Food Floor. But that day, instead of the usual tables for pizzas, burgers, and burritos, the space had been cleared out, except for a band, which was tuning up noisily.

Dozens of kids were busily laying out banners. Soon, hand-lettered messages like Youth for Walker and Bayport Supports Walker for Prez! covered the walls. The band members looked around. "Ready?" one asked.

The kids working on the banners nodded.

With amps cranked up to max, the band launched into an old Elvis number. But instead of the usual lyrics, there were new words pushing Philip Walker's candidacy.

The music blasted up to the roof, echoing in the huge open space. Heads began appearing, staring down, along the safety railings that lined the shopping levels. Still more shoppers gathered on the Food Floor. Callie, Iola, and four other kids circulated through the crowd, handing out leaflets.

Even the local congressman showed up, making a speech for Walker. "And remember," he finished, "this rally is only the dress rehearsal. Come back next week for a bigger and better show, with a special guest star—Philip Walker himself!"

The Food Floor was packed with people cheering and applauding. But Frank Hardy backed away, turned off by all the hype. Since he'd lost Joe after about five seconds in the jostling mob, he fought his way to the edges of the crowd, trying to spot him.

Joe was leaning against one of the many pillars supporting the mall. He had a big grin on his face and was talking with a gorgeous blond girl. Frank hurried over to them. But Joe, deep in conversation with his new friend, didn't notice his brother. More importantly, he didn't notice his girlfriend making her way through the crowd.

Frank arrived about two steps behind Iola, who had wrapped one arm around Joe's waist while glaring at the blond. "Oh, uh, hi," said Joe, his grin fading in embarrassment. "This is Val. She just came—"

"I'd love to stay and talk," Iola said, cutting Joe off, "but we have a problem. We're running out of leaflets. The only ones left are on the backseat of your car. Could you help me get them?"

"Right now? We just got here," Joe complained.

"Yeah, and I can see you're really busy," Iola said, looking at Val. "Are you coming?"

Joe hesitated for a moment, looking from Iola to the blond girl. "Okay." His hand fished around in his pocket and came out with his car keys. "I'll be with you in a minute, okay?" He started playing catch with the keys, tossing them in the air as he turned back to Val.

But Iola angrily snatched the keys in midair. Then she rushed off, nearly knocking Frank over.

"Hey, Joe, I've got to talk to you," Frank said, smiling at Val as he took his brother by the elbow. "Excuse us a second." He pulled Joe around the pillar.

"What's going on?" Joe complained. "I can't even start a friendly conversation without everybody jumping on me."

"You know, it's lucky you're so good at picking up girls," said Frank. "Because you sure are tough on the ones you already know."

Joe's face went red. "What are you talking about?"

"You know what I'm talking about. I saw your little trick with the keys there a minute ago. You made Iola look like a real jerk in front of some girl you've been hitting on. Make up your mind, Joe. Is Iola your girlfriend or not?"

Joe seemed to be studying the toes of his running shoes as Frank spoke. "You're right, I guess," he finally muttered. "But I was gonna go! Why did she have to make such a life-and-death deal out of it?"

Frank grinned. "It's your fatal charm, Joe. It stirs up women's passions."

"Very funny." Joe sighed. "So what should I do?"

"Let's go out to the car and give Iola a hand," Frank suggested. "She can't handle that big box all by herself."

He put his head around the pillar and smiled at Val. "Sorry. I have to borrow this guy for a while. We'll be back in a few minutes."

They headed for the nearest exit. The sleek, modern mall decor gave way to painted cinderblocks as they headed down the corridor to the underground parking garages. "We should've caught up to her by now," Joe said as they came to the first row of cars. "She must be really steamed."

He was glancing around for Iola, but the underground lot was a perfect place for hide-and-seek. Every ten feet or so, squat concrete pillars which supported the upper levels rose from the floor, blocking the view. But as the Hardys reached the end of the row of cars, they saw a dark-haired figure marching angrily ahead of them.

"Iola!" Joe called.

Instead of turning around, Iola put on speed.

"Hey, Iola, wait a minute!" Joe picked up his pace, but Iola darted around a pillar. A second later she'd disappeared.

"Calm down," Frank said. "She'll be outside at the car. You can talk to her then."

Joe led the way to the outdoor parking lot, nervously pacing ahead of Frank. "She's really angry," he said as they stepped outside. "I just hope she doesn't—"

The explosion drowned out whatever he was going to say. They ran to the spot where they'd parked their yellow sedan. But the car—and Iola—had erupted in a ball of white-hot flame!

# Chapter
## 2

"FRANK! WAIT UP!"

Hearing his name, Frank Hardy turned to see Callie Shaw walking quickly along the sidewalk. He stood and waited, glad for one more excuse to delay going into the funeral chapel.

Dressed in a suit, with his dark hair neatly combed, Frank didn't look at all like the guy in jeans and sneakers who'd slugged it out with Joe all over the parking lot two days before. Only a closer look at his lean face showed the remains of a split lip and the fatigue smudges under his eyes.

Callie took his arm and matched strides with him. "Why are you here alone?" she asked. "Where's Joe?"

"Inside—I think. I haven't seen him since early this morning." Frank's face was tight. "But

I heard him all last night, pacing around his room."

Frank reached over to take Callie's hand. "The whole family seems to be going crazy. Dad looked like he'd seen a ghost when the cops finally brought us home. He told us to stay in the house, then locked himself in the den, making phone calls. Now he's disappeared. Maybe it has something to do with this case."

"He didn't tell you anything?" Callie asked.

"I saw Dad for about two minutes last night." The frustration was clear in Frank's voice as they headed up the walk to the quiet, white-painted chapel. "He was carrying his suitcase to the car. All he said was that I should apologize to the Mortons and represent the family today. Mom and Aunt Gertrude are supposed to stay at the house. Something to do with all those phone calls."

Callie squeezed his hand. "Frank, it all sounds so weird."

He shook his head as they reached the chapel door. "I know. It's crazy. The cops are saying somebody planted a bomb in the car. But there's nothing to go on. No clues, nothing."

They froze in the doorway when they caught sight of the broad-shouldered figure sitting in the last row of seats. "I don't think I've ever seen Joe in a suit," Callie whispered. "He looks like a different person."

"He's *acting* like a different person," Frank

whispered back. "Did you ever see him sit anywhere for five minutes without tapping his fingers
or shifting around?"

But Joe remained unnaturally still. When
Frank and Callie stopped beside him, he didn't
turn. His face looked as if it were carved out of
marble, as pale as his white shirt. His smile lines
had been erased. Staring at the front of the
chapel, he didn't even notice Frank and Callie.

"I guess he really did love Iola, in spite of his
wandering eye," Callie said quietly.

"I suppose. He hasn't said anything since the
explosion. For the first time in our lives, I can't
get him to speak to me." The strain showed on
Frank's face.

The service itself was brief—all about Iola
being taken "in the flower of her youth." No one
touched on the fact that she'd been killed. There
was no mention of bombs or police investiga-
tions.

Then the people in the chapel filed out, offering
condolences to Mr. and Mrs. Morton and to
Chet, Iola's older brother. Frank held his breath
as Joe approached the Mortons.

"I—I can't tell you how sorry . . ." Joe began.
"If I had known—if I could . . ." He choked,
turning abruptly to Frank. "Help me get out of
here," he whispered.

Frank took his brother's arm and headed for
the door. Joe was quivering like a machine on
overload that was about to fly apart. Frank had to

get him into the open so he could let off steam.

But a short figure stood silhouetted in the door-way, blocking their path. "Frank and Joe Hardy?" it said.

The boys stopped in surprise. The person be-fore them was a stranger, the most ordinary-looking man they'd ever seen. From his balding head to his black lace-up shoes, he virtually screamed, "Don't remember me!" Reaching in-side a slightly rumpled raincoat, the little gray man said, "I'm sorry. Let me introduce myself."

He pulled two cards out of his pocket. Frank took one. "Arthur E. Gray," he read, "World Import–Export."

"My firm is a client of your father's," Gray explained.

"He's never mentioned you," said Frank.

"Ah, but Fenton Hardy has often spoken of his sons," Gray said. "And since I was in town when this sad event took place, I wanted to offer my condolences." He looked at Joe. "This must be especially hard for you."

Joe managed a nod. But Frank saw that his brother was just barely restraining himself from ramming the guy out of his way. As Gray stood blathering on, Frank dropped a hand onto Joe's arm.

"Well, it was, uh, very nice of you to speak with us," Frank said, "but we shouldn't be block-ing the door—"

The man stuck with them. "I have a car," he said. "If you need a lift home . . ."

Silent warning bells began going off in Frank's head. A complete stranger claims to be an associate of Dad's and offers us a ride. Maybe the guy is legit, he thought. But after someone has just blown up our car, it doesn't seem like a good idea.

"Thanks just the same, but we'd rather walk for a bit—kind of clear our minds," Frank said.

For a second, something flickered in the man's eyes. Then he nodded, adding, "I understand that your father isn't in town right now. Please feel free to call on me for anything." He pressed the cards on both of them. "You can reach me by dialing this number. Just ask for Mr. Gray."

Frank and Joe said their goodbyes and headed into a nearby park. "Who *was* that bozo?" Joe muttered.

"I wish Dad were around so we could ask him," Frank said.

Joe glanced at his brother as they walked through the park. "Where do you think Dad went?"

"I'm not sure," Frank replied. "You know he was working on a big case—top secret all the way. Maybe it's that." He faltered for a second. "Or maybe it's Iola."

"Yeah," said Joe. He stopped in the middle of the path. "We have to talk."

"I was wondering if we'd ever do that again." Frank stood looking at his brother.

Joe looked away. "I spent a lot of time thinking. About me, and about Iola."

"Joe—"

"All last night, I kept seeing her," Joe said. "She was so pretty, so delicate." His hands bunched into fists. "How did she ever wind up with a guy like me? All the stupid stunts I pulled . . ."

"You didn't know what was going to happen," Frank said. "You can't keep blaming yourself."

"I'm going to get whoever did this," Joe broke in. "And when I'm through, he'll wish he'd never been born."

The good-natured face that had cracked a thousand jokes was gone. The new Joe Hardy was a stranger, his expression cold and hard as a statue's. But his eyes were alive with a light that promised lethal action.

"Know where I was this morning?" he went on. "Back at the mall. The cops had just about finished looking for evidence. But I talked to a couple of bomb experts.

"As far as they can figure out, the whole car was filled with plastic explosive. The guy even put a detonator in the gas tank, to make sure it went up. There was hardly anything left of the car, much less Iola. The guy who did this ought to be squashed like a bug."

"Joe—"

With choppy motions, Joe ripped off his tie. "You say I shouldn't blame myself, *but it was my fault*. I can't forget that. Remember these?" He pulled a chain out of his shirt.

On it were a pair of keys, twisted and melted together. The last time Frank had seen them, they'd been jingling in midair, with Iola's hand grabbing for them.

Joe tucked them back inside his collar. "I'm keeping them to remind me that we've got work to do. Somebody's got to pay. Are you with me?"

"Are you kidding?" said Frank. "We're in this together. And don't forget that."

For the first time that day, Joe Hardy smiled. "Okay. So where do we start?"

"The cops," Frank responded.

The Bayport police station was on Main Street, a short walk from the park. It was a solid, old-fashioned brick building with an old-fashioned brick jailhouse in the back. As the Hardys walked up the worn stone steps, they were greeted by a friendly face. It belonged to Officer Con Riley.

"Con?" Frank asked. "Who's handling the Morton case?"

"That's the new guy," Riley responded. "Butler. He's supposed to be a real hotshot, with a big arrest record for the NYPD."

"A hotshot detective from New York, huh?" said Joe. "Let's go in and check this guy out."

The boys walked through the offices of the Detective Division, and Joe knocked on a door labeled s. BUTLER—DETECTIVE INSPECTOR.

The desk inside was piled high with papers, and behind them sat a tall, black-haired man. His tanned face was long and thin, his eyes so dark they looked black. He stared at them, poker-faced, until he heard Frank and Joe's names. Then his eyes narrowed.

"Well, you saved me the trouble of calling you downtown," he said crisply. "Maybe you'll smarten up and confess." His stern, unmoving face swiveled between Frank and Joe. "I want to know what you two clowns had in that car, because whatever it was makes you responsible for Iola Morton's murder!"

# Chapter
## 3

JOE'S FACE TURNED pale, then brick red. "Are you accusing us . . . ?" He was so angry his voice choked off.

Butler looked him straight in the eye. "Did you really think I'd fall for that ridiculous mad-bomber story? Nobody would waste a bomb on a pair of punk kids. But punk kids playing with the wrong toys might blow themselves up. Especially kids who get involved in politics."

"If you're trying to make us look like a pair of political crazies, maybe you should talk to Chief Collig." Frank's voice was quiet but icy. "We've worked on cases for him. He knows us."

"Oh, *sure*. I heard this song all the time in New York." Butler's lips started to twist into a sneer; then the poker face slid on, almost as if it hurt him to show any expression. "Human slime with

17

important friends to cover for them. Even if they're caught red-handed, there're always people to say, 'Oh, Inspector, they're really good boys.' That does *not* impress me."

Joe's rage finally found a voice. "You do a real terrifying tough cop. Where do you get those lines? Watching 'Kojak' reruns?"

For a moment, Butler gave him a blank, almost startled stare. "Never mind where I get my 'lines,' " he snapped. "Just remember this. I hear you two go around playing junior detectives. Well, don't get in my way. You're my prime suspects right now.

"If I catch either of you muddying up the waters, I'll arrest you for impeding an investigation. I'll do it so fast your heads will spin. And it won't do any good to go whining to your important friends to bail you out."

The corners of Butler's mouth went up two millimeters in the faintest of smiles. "I'm sure I'll have questions for you as I go on . . . lots of questions. And it goes without saying—don't leave town."

He turned back to the papers on his desk, as if the Hardys had disappeared.

Joe followed his brother through the office door, slamming it behind him. "That miserable—" He bit off the rest of what he was going to say. "Well, I can see that the cops are gonna be a *lot* of help!" He glared at Frank. "So what's our next brilliant move?"

"We borrow a car and head for the mall." Only Frank's eyes showed his anger.

"But that guy just said—"

"I know," Frank interrupted with a grin. "And I can't think of a better place to start impeding his investigation."

Joe insisted that they check out the parking lot, even though it had been cleared of wreckage. "There's nothing," Frank said, looking at the large scorched spot on the concrete.

"Then why are we here?"

"We want to see if anyone remembers anything odd about Saturday—anything out of the ordinary."

"Out of the ordinary!" Joe burst out. "There was a *political rally* going on! How much more out of the ordinary do you want? Besides," he said, "the Saturday shoppers are long gone. How are we going to question them?"

"We're not," Frank replied. "I want to talk to the people who are always here—the store owners. They'd be the ones to notice something—or some*one*—out of place."

Their first stop on entering the mall was Mr. Pizza. The fast-food joint was the prime hangout, and the manager was an old school friend of theirs, Tony Prito.

Tony's cheerful grin wavered for an instant when he saw the Hardys. He stepped out from behind the counter, grabbing Joe's hand. "I didn't get a chance to talk to you at the chapel," he said as he led them to a table and they sat down. "Have they caught whoever was behind it?"

"I don't think the cops even have a clue." Joe scowled.

"It's hard to figure out *who* blew up the car if you don't know *why,*" Frank said.

"Well, it was your car," Tony pointed out.

"Right. But was the bomb aimed at us?" Frank shook his head. "That's the question. For all we know, it could have been a random thing, some nut who just blows up yellow sedans."

"Yeah, but there are a lot of guys who might want to get back at you—or your father." Tony smiled. "Detectives who put people away aren't popular with crooks."

"I got Dad's assistant working on that angle this morning," Frank said. "He's checking to see if anyone who might have a grudge against us was recently released."

"Wait a second," Joe burst out. "Maybe the bomber knew that Iola and Callie were with us. Maybe he—or she—had a grudge against the Mortons or the Shaws."

He thought for a moment. "And the bomb was set in the middle of a political rally. Could the person have something against the Walker campaign?" He shook his head. "But Frank and I didn't even know there was going to be a rally.

We didn't know we were going to be at the mall. This doesn't make sense."

"Tell me about it," Frank agreed sarcastically. "Here's the thing I can't figure out—why the mall? If I were going to blow somebody up, I'd do it right in front of the person's house—a nice, unmistakable message. Why would this guy follow us to a crowded parking lot to do the job? It's got to have something to do with the mall." He looked up at Tony. "Were the cops around asking questions?"

"They gave us the once-over lightly. I was kind of surprised." Tony shrugged. "Maybe they'll be back today."

"Well, we want to ask some questions *now*," Joe said, leaning over the table. "Think you can give us a hand, Tony? Introduce us to some of the store owners?"

"Sure. Most of them come down here to get a slice for lunch. Hey, Jean," he called to the girl behind the counter, "I'm taking an early break. Be back in five minutes."

Tony led the Hardys up the mall escalators to the first floor of shops, then into the Builder's Paradise hardware store. "Dan Stone runs this place. He's a good guy, and he's president of the Mall Association. You can get all the help you need from him."

Stone turned out to be a friendly man in his late thirties. He was only too eager to help, and the

Hardys spent most of the next two hours talking to store owners. None of them had noticed anything other than the bedlam of the political rally, but lots of them had things to say about the mall. Frank mentioned it as they took a shortcut to their car through Lacey's department store.

"Did you notice how many of those people complained about the security?" Frank stopped beside a mannequin in a low-cut gown to pull out his notebook.

"Do we have to stop here? It looks like you're trying to get that dummy's phone number," Joe said.

Frank paid no attention. "Every store owner we spoke to says he or she is being ripped off. Look at this list. Hundreds of feet of wire missing from the Audio-Video Den. Electric clocks disappearing from the Gifte Shoppe. Mr. Stone losing wire clippers, electrical supplies . . ." Frank suddenly went silent. "That's all stuff you'd need to build bombs."

Joe stopped dead in his tracks. As he turned to his brother, he felt a tiny tug on the sleeve of his jacket. A flash of movement caught his eye, a glittering something that cut through his jacket, whizzed past him, and stuck with a dull thud in the mannequin's plaster "flesh."

His breath caught in his throat as he stared at the silvery dart quivering in the dummy's chest. "It tore right through—"

Frank grabbed his arm. "Let's get out of here before they try another shot!"

Joe followed his brother, looking over his shoulder at the people around them. A typical mall crowd, hundreds of shoppers clogging the aisles—except that one of those "shoppers" was trying to kill them!

# Chapter
## 4

THEY FOUGHT THEIR way through a mass of people, all intent on their shopping and hardly suspecting that a silent killer stalked among them. Frank turned back to Joe as they reached the men's department. "Spot anyone following us?" he asked.

"Too many people," Joe responded, scanning the crowd. "But I don't—"

Another dart hissed between them, burying itself into a pile of sport shirts. Joe banged his fist in frustration.

"Come on!" he snapped, muscling his way through the crowd, moving like a broken-field runner as he raced for the nearest exit. Frank kept close on his brother's heels, ignoring the annoyed looks he got from jostled shoppers.

He threw a glance over his shoulder as they

drew near the exit and the crowd thinned. There was still no trace of the mysterious gunman. Joe took advantage of the empty space to break into a run.

Before they reached the door, however, a store security guard bustled into their path. "Hold it, you kids. What do you think—" A silvery streak whizzed past them just as the guard brought a walkie-talkie to his lips. The man jerked back a step, stared in surprise at the dart sticking out of the shoulder of his red security blazer, then collapsed without a word.

Joe started to lean over the man, but Frank pushed him toward the door. "That's just what they want you to do. Go!"

They burst out the door, and Frank bolted off to the left. "There's the movie theater! If we make it around that corner—"

"*If!*" Joe burst out, running hard on Frank's heels. The corner was at least fifty yards away, at the end of a plain concrete wall that gave no cover at all—not even a planter stand. "Great escape route, Frank."

"Save your breath for running," his brother replied.

Behind them, the boys heard screams and hubbub, people responding to the sight of the collapsed guard. With luck, maybe a crowd would gather, blocking the door and giving them a few more seconds' lead.

Joe's legs pumped, bringing him almost even

with Frank. It was like a nightmare. He was running as fast as he could, but that corner didn't seem to be coming any closer. And behind them . . . surely by now the guy with the gun had reached the door of the department store.

The muscles between Joe's shoulder blades bunched in tension, expecting the sting of a dart to tear into them at any moment. He started to turn his head. If anyone was going to shoot him, Joe Hardy was going to look his killer in the eye.

Frank must have picked up the change of rhythm in Joe's footfalls. "Don't turn! . . . Almost . . . corner." He gasped out the words.

Joe's head snapped forward. Sure enough, there was the corner! He poured on an added burst of speed, feeling his own breath burning in his throat, and then he was beside Frank, making the turn, just as another dart chipped the concrete at the corner.

Frank slowed down slightly once they had the cover of the wall behind them. He staggered a little as he led the way across a parking lot and up to the mall's six-plex movie theater.

"Good thinking," Joe wheezed. "With a dozen theaters to hide in, we're sure to lose this guy."

"Yeah," Frank said. "But how about this? If the guy chases us into the theater, he's walking blind into a pitch-black room—"

"And that gives us a chance to turn the tables on him," Joe finished. "Perfect!"

They reached the box office, and Frank

dragged out his wallet, scanning the title board. "Uh, two for the Bond movie revival—Theater Five."

"But the film is almost half over," the ticket seller said.

"That's okay. We just want to catch the ending." Frank grinned at her as he shoved a couple of bills under the partition. He glanced back at Joe. "Our friend arrive yet?"

Joe had a quick impression of sunglasses, a black leather jacket, and jeans as their pursuer came around the corner, then jerked back. "He's here, but he's not coming into the open."

"Well, he's seen us. Let's make sure he sees where we're going." Frank took the tickets from the girl and headed swiftly into the theater.

"I picked Theater Five because it's the smallest," Frank explained as they handed their tickets to the usher. "If we're going to have a roughhouse, I don't want to give him much room to move around in."

As soon as they had slipped through the soundproofed doors of Theater Five, they were hit with blaringly loud sixties music. On the screen above them, Sean Connery was swinging a length of pipe at a heavy, muscular guy. Even though Connery was swinging with all his might, it didn't seem to faze his enemy.

"Turn away from the screen," Frank whispered. "We want our eyes to be used to the dark when this guy comes in. That means we've got eight seconds while he'll be effectively blind—enough time to ambush him."

They positioned themselves on either side of the door and waited. Finally the door swung open, and a man stepped into the theater. The screen wasn't radiating much light, so they couldn't see his face. But even in the fuzzy darkness they could see the gun in the man's hand.

Frank struck first, his hand hurtling down like a blade onto the man's wrist. The gun flew from his grasp. Joe stepped in, throwing a punch at the man's stomach.

But even as Joe swung, the man twisted aside, driving his elbow into the pit of Frank's stomach. Frank folded, and the man launched a killing blow to Frank's neck, a blow that missed as Joe kicked desperately into the back of the guy's leg.

The leg buckled, but the man launched a clawlike finger at Joe's throat. Joe hunched his shoulders and landed a solid punch into his assailant's face. The man staggered back, and Joe charged forward, butting with his head and knocking him to the floor. Joe jumped for a pin-down.

Even trapped on his back, the man continued to fight like a demon, trying to wriggle loose. A vicious blow to the bridge of Joe's nose had him seeing stars. He recoiled slightly, and his captive nearly twisted free.

Joe slugged him again, and then they were

grappling. Above them, the film music reached a crescendo, drowning out their grunts of effort.

Frank Hardy scrabbled frantically along the darkened aisle, trying to find the dart gun.

Then the theater doors opened again, and Frank saw another male figure—aiming another dart gun. "Joe! Down!" he screamed. He threw himself, knocking Joe flat just as the dart flew over their heads.

"Wha—?" Joe said, dazed. "I thought you were on my side."

Frank pointed at the outline of the new player in the game, who was already loading another dart into his gun.

"Uh-oh," his brother said. "Let's get out of here."

"You going to ask him politely to step aside?" Joe asked as Frank hauled him to his feet.

"I'd say this was an emergency. Let's use the emergency exit."

The soundtrack had grown much quieter, and movie patrons started turning around at the sound of voices behind them. "Shut up, you're ruining the flick!" A few even stood up and turned around. "What's going on back there?"

"Let's get moving before they block the aisle." Frank took off at full speed toward the screen, with Joe right behind him.

"Down in front!" patrons began to scream as the Hardys blocked their view, rushing toward the screen. Above them was a huge close-up of

Sean Connery, his face twisted in a grimace of rage. Just ahead of them was the Exit sign.

Together, the Hardys hit the panic bar on the door, smashing it open. They tumbled through the emergency exit, out into brilliant sunlight.

"Come on!" Frank lurched into the parking lot, half-blinded. But three steps from the exit, he crashed into something. He stepped back, blinking, and then froze. Blocking their retreat was a long black car, rear doors open.

"Get in," a cold, hard voice commanded.

# Chapter

# 5

FRANK AND JOE hesitated just an instant—until a dart scored the paint on the fender beside them. "No choice," Frank said.

He and Joe got into the car. The door closed behind them, muffling the noise as the vehicle screeched away from the curb.

"What's going on?" said Frank in surprise. "I thought those guys were coming along."

"Looks like they thought so, too," Joe said, glancing out the rear windshield. Two figures sprinted from the theater emergency exit. One aimed a pistol, and they saw the gleam of a dart fly at them and bounce off the trunk of the car.

The smoked-glass partition hiding the front seat rolled down with a whirring noise, bringing both Hardys' heads front. "Don't jump to conclusions until you know all the facts, boys," said the driver of the car, turning around.

Frank and Joe sat in shock, staring at Arthur Gray.

"What are *you* doing here?" Joe finally managed to say.

"Rescuing you," Gray replied, turning back to the road. "From the looks of things, I arrived just in time."

"Yeah," Frank said, suspicion in his voice. "You came along very conveniently. *Too* conveniently."

Gray smiled as he glanced in the rearview mirror. "I took the liberty of keeping a discreet electronic eye on you."

"How?" Frank demanded.

"Remember those cards I gave you? They're not cardboard, they're plastic. And inside they're marvels of microelectronics."

"You *bugged* us?" Joe burst out.

"Not exactly. They're locator devices. We could plot your movements. When your movements suddenly became rather erratic, we knew something was up. So I came to collect you. And you're right. I'd say it was *very* convenient that I came along."

The car had pulled out of the parking area, and Gray poured on the speed.

"You know, I've had just about enough of this cloak-and-dagger stuff," Frank said.

Gray didn't turn or even respond.

"I want to know what's going on here. And I want it straight."

Still Gray didn't answer.

"Kind of tough, arguing with the back of somebody's head," Joe commented.

"Do you hear me?" Frank said, reaching out to grab the man by the shoulder.

Before Frank's hand reached the front seat, the glass divider came up like a reverse guillotine. Startled, Frank jerked his hand back. The divider rolled back down.

"Sorry about that," Gray apologized. "Security measure. Although I am a bit surprised. Our files said your brother was the hot-headed one."

"Ah, come on, give him a break," Joe said.

Frank was staring. "Files?" he repeated. "Just who are you?"

"Let's say I'm connected with the intelligence community," the Gray Man replied.

"CIA?"

The government man shook his head. "Nothing so crude. The Network does more . . . delicate . . . information gathering."

"The Network, huh? CBS instead of CIA?" Frank was having a tough time accepting Gray's transformation from nerd to secret agent. His eyes narrowed in thought. "So that story about your company being a client of Dad's, that was all phony." He stared at the man. "I suppose even the name on the card isn't real."

"It's close to my code name," the government agent said. "Gray Man. World Import–Export exists. It's a cover company for the Network.

And your father has given us some help from time to time. That's why I'm here. He's called in some favors, wants his family kept safely out of sight."

"While he does what?" Frank asked.

"I've got people trying to find that out," the Gray Man replied. He took a deep breath, as if wondering where to begin. "It all revolves around the Walker campaign."

Joe stared. "You mean Iola was blown up because she supported Philip Walker?"

"No." The Gray Man shook his head. "We're pretty sure that bomb was aimed at you—and, through you, at your father. He's head of security for Philip Walker's campaign."

"So *that's* the big job he's been so tight-lipped about," Frank said.

The Gray Man nodded. "And it's turned into a bigger job since Walker began talking about terrorists. Certain groups weren't happy about that. They were even less happy when your father began gathering information on them."

He looked back at the Hardys. "You see, Fenton Hardy got lucky. He got a line on a group nobody's been able to crack—the Assassins."

Joe laughed. "Sounds like a cycle gang."

The Gray Man didn't crack a smile. "These are very, very dangerous men. They started as a bunch of fanatics in the days of the Crusades. And they've stayed in the business of terrorism ever since—almost a thousand years of experience.

"They hire themselves out nowadays, and they use the most modern technology. The bomb that blasted your car, for instance—the local police are still scratching their heads over it."

"But we still don't understand why they did it," Frank said.

"To silence your father," the Gray Man answered. "Your father found out about a major Assassin project, a series of terrorist attacks in cities all across America. They wanted to scare him into silence or, even better, use him for their own propaganda."

"They don't know Dad very well," Joe said.

"Probably not. But they trust to their own motto—Kill one, frighten a hundred. And they're usually right. They needed Fenton Hardy. They couldn't threaten him, but they could threaten his family. And to show they meant business, they blew you up."

"Except they didn't get us." Joe's voice was hard. "They got Iola."

"Well, that explains why Dad got so grim after the bombing," Frank said. "It explains his quick disappearance, too." He turned to the Gray Man. "He's gone underground, trying to use his connection to the Assassins, hasn't he? But wait a second! What about that threat? That means Mom and Aunt Gertrude are in danger."

"Your mother and your aunt are with our agents," the Gray Man explained. "They're already out of Bayport, headed for a secret destination." He smiled. "We'll be doing the same with you. We have a nice Marine base in South Carolina picked out for you."

"No way!" Joe replied heatedly. "I want the guy who set that bomb. And that means I've got to be in Bayport, not boot camp."

"Look, sonny, I don't care what you want." The Gray Man didn't even look away from the road. "We're keeping you under wraps until the case is closed."

"Will you be staying on Iola's case?" Frank asked.

"The Assassins are my case," said the Gray Man. "I've got a lead that their headquarters is now in London. That's where I'll be headed after I drop you off."

"Drop us where?" Joe's voice was raw with rebelliousness.

"At your home, of course. Our people will meet you there, and you'll be on your way."

"You're not going to ship me off someplace! Pull over," Joe said, reaching for the door handle. "I'm getting out here!"

The Gray Man glanced at them in the rearview mirror as he pulled onto the gravel shoulder. They were on a quiet secondary road, two lanes of blacktop in the middle of a scene that looked more like country than suburbs.

No one was around. Even the road was deserted, except for a telephone repair van that disappeared in a dip in the road behind them.

"Listen, kid," the Gray Man began as Joe struggled furiously with the door handle.

"Look, I'm not a kid. I've made up my mind. So stop screwing around with these locks and let me out!"

"You're not leaving," the government man growled, turning in his seat. "Get that clear."

At that moment, the telephone van appeared behind them, putting on speed. It came abreast of the car, then swerved onto the shoulder ahead of them. The back door flew open, revealing a masked figure with an Uzi submachine gun in his hands.

As the Hardys watched in horror, he emptied half the clip of his gun point-blank into their windshield.

# Chapter
## 6

FRANK AND JOE sat frozen as a dozen bullets hit the windshield and ricocheted off.

The Gray Man let out a long breath. "Another security feature—bulletproof glass," he said, watching the van pull off ahead of them. "They'd need a bazooka to hurt us."

"Y-you might have mentioned that earlier," Frank said, trying to get control of his voice.

No answer from the Gray Man. He was dialing a number on a cellular phone on the dashboard. "We're about four miles along the Interstate. Hostiles attacking. Get some backup here to intercept." He hung up with a smile. "Nothing more to worry about."

The van had roared down the road about a hundred yards. Now it whipped around in a tight U-turn and came careening back toward them.

"What would happen if those guys tried to ram us?" Joe asked.

"Let's not find out," the Gray Man replied, gunning the engine. From a standing start, the car shot forward, but it wasn't entirely out of the way when the van barreled up from behind.

A sideswipe sent their car fishtailing down the road as the Gray Man fought the wheel. They'd turned almost halfway around before he was back in control.

Meanwhile, the van shrieked around in another U-turn, coming for them again.

"They'll catch us broadside!" Frank yelled.

The Gray Man twisted the wheel and tromped hard on the accelerator. Squealing tires left long rubber tracks on the road as the car whirled around and peeled out.

But the van was too close to escape. It smashed into the rear of the car, sending everyone lurching. Twice more it approached and rammed, coming close enough to give the Hardys a clear view of the driver. Although his face was masked, they could see the fanatical gleam in his eyes.

He was joined by a second figure, the machine-gunner from the rear of the van. He leaned out the side window, firing the Uzi one-handed. The burst wasn't accurate; he was merely hosing the car with bullets.

"They can't hurt us with that," said the Gray Man, flinching as a stream of slugs smacked into the windows. "But they certainly are distract-ing."

Now the van pulled abreast of the car, trying to force it off the road. The car bounced to the shoulder, throwing out a stream of gravel as its tires howled in protest. For a second it was off the road completely. Then the Gray Man pulled it back onto the pavement—only to find the van had turned again and was coming at them head-on!

"It's like a game of chicken," Joe muttered as he watched the now dented front end of the van loom closer. "Only this guy isn't going to back off."

The van ate up the distance between them as the Gray Man tried desperate evasive maneuvers. He headed left, but the van drifted into his path. He aimed right, but the van moved to intercept again.

Faking left, then right, the Gray Man pushed the pedal to the floor. The car shot forward, swerving left yet again. For one horrible instant the van loomed before them, then they were past it, but they still took a glancing blow that left the car teetering on two wheels. For a second it hung there, about to flip over; then it bounced back to the road with a bone-jarring impact.

"I've had just about enough of this," the Gray Man said through gritted teeth, reaching for something mounted under the dashboard. His hand returned with a Browning automatic pistol. "Can either of you handle this?"

Joe took the heavy gun, hefting it. "Dad always makes us practice on the firing range," he said. "I'm the better shot."

He looked at the Gray Man. "But do you think it's a good idea to open a window with that Uzi out there?"

"No need." The Gray Man's fingers flicked over the dashboard, and a whirring noise filled the car. Joe turned to see a thin slit appearing in the rear windshield. "Gunport," the government man explained.

Joe already had the pistol out, tracking the van. One shot, and a star-shaped set of cracks appeared in the windshield between driver and passenger.

"Uh, Joe, we'd like them alive for questioning, if possible," said the Gray Man.

"Okay." But his second shot missed completely as the van swerved violently. The third went into the body of the van.

"I think you'll have a hard time knocking the engine out," the Gray Man said.

The gunner in the van slammed a new clip into his Uzi and sprayed the rear windshield, trying to hit the gunport.

Frank held his breath as bullets splattered closer and closer to the open slit. But Joe remained absolutely calm, taking his time as he aimed.

"How about this?" he said, squeezing the trigger.

The right front tire of the van exploded as his bullet hit home. While the driver struggled frantically, the van went into an uncontrollable skid—across the road, onto the gravel shoulder, then tumbling onto its side in an err.pty field.

Joe handed the Browning back, smiling grimly. "Two down."

Frank's face was thoughtful as he looked at the overturned van. "I wonder how many more there'll be."

"*I* wonder what we're going to do about those two guys out there," Joe said. "I don't think they're going anywhere. But I wouldn't like the idea of having to face that machine gun."

The Gray Man was already on the car phone. "I'll pass the warning on to our backup. They can take care of it," he said. "They'll also clear everything with the local police."

"Speaking of the local police," Frank said, "you've got something else to clear—us. The police seem to think we're prime suspects in Iola's death." He went over their interrogation by Inspector Butler. "He doesn't want us to leave town, so he may get a little upset if he hears we've disappeared." Frank smiled. "Not that I'm against the idea of upsetting him."

"Everything will be straightened out," the Gray Man said. "We can take care of it."

They turned off the Interstate at the next exit. Moments later, they were driving through the tall trees and old-fashioned houses of the Hardys' neighborhood. Although Frank and Joe's house looked empty, the Gray Man went in with them, holding on to the Browning in his raincoat pocket. "All clear," he said after checking out the house. "My people will be here in a few minutes. Don't let anyone in unless they mention my code name."

" 'The Gray Man sent me,' " Frank said.

As soon as the government man had left, Joe turned to his brother. "You're not really gonna sit around here and let his friends take us to Carolina, are you?"

"I didn't say that," Frank said, heading into the den. "I only promised not to open the door to strangers, like any good five-year-old would do."

"So what are you doing hanging around?" Joe asked as his brother warmed up the family computer. "We've got to get out of here."

"We need a place to go, first," Frank answered, putting the modem on-line. "And from what the Gray Man said, that place is London."

*"What?"* cried Joe.

"We don't have any clues here, and if we want to stay in Bayport, we'll have to hide." Frank looked up at Joe as his fingers danced over the computer keyboard. "That's not the best way to run an investigation. . . . Ah!"

" 'Ah' what?" Joe asked.

"I'm in the airport reservations computer. It's not easy getting in, but a friend of mine showed me how."

Joe stared. "I thought you hated hacking!"

"This time it's for a good cause." Frank hit more keys. "There's only one direct flight to London in the next few hours, and here's the passenger list." He scanned the screen. "What a surprise. Mr. Arthur Gray." His fingers resumed dancing all over the keyboard.

"Frank, what are you doing?"

"Entering our reservations and selecting our seats. You'd better dig out our passports."

Joe was still staring. "But how are we going to pay for all this?"

Frank got up from the computer. "Plastic. Dad gave us credit cards to cover unforeseen contingencies. Well, what do you call this?"

"But *London* . . ."

"I made it as cheap as possible," Frank said, heading for the door. "We're only booked one-way." He stopped in the doorway, grinning at Joe. "Well, come on, pack a bag. We've got to get out of here."

Shortly afterward, the Hardys stood at the airport security checkpoint. They'd picked up their tickets, and their bags had already been X-rayed. But a delay developed when an elderly couple—a man pushing a woman in a wheelchair—approached the metal detector gate.

"Now what do they do about that?" Joe asked. "The metal in the chair will set the alarm off."

He watched as the airport security people

44

wheeled the old woman off to the side. "Look at that," he said, fascinated. "They're *frisking* her!"

The security officers were thorough, even checking the pillow on the seat of the wheelchair for contraband.

"Well, I guess she's okay," Joe said.

"Yeah, she wasn't sitting on a shotgun or anything," Frank responded in a solemn voice.

Joe laughed.

"Quiet. Now let's see what happens to the lady's escort."

"Me?" the elderly man said to the guards. "I'm only seeing Martha onto the plane."

Frank grinned as the security people waved him past the gate. "I think we've just learned an important lesson here, Joe. If you want to smuggle something into an airport, carry it yourself while pushing a wheelchair."

They walked through the detector and rushed for their departure gate. The boarding announcement for their flight was already being broadcast over the airport loudspeakers. They reached the gate and found the old woman being wheeled aboard the plane ahead of everyone else.

What do you know? Old Martha is heading for London! Frank thought. He followed the flow of people into the gate and noticed that the old man (her husband?) was being allowed to accompany his wife onto the plane. Frank shrugged and filed after Joe.

As he entered the plane, he saw Martha being seated by the old gent in the very first seats of the cabin, just behind the cockpit door. Then Frank and his brother reached the seats Frank had reserved—right beside the Gray Man.

Frank thought the government agent was going to have a stroke when he saw them. "You two!" he sputtered.

"We thought you'd like the company," Joe said.

"And London is so beautiful this time of year," Frank added. "So much nicer than Carolina."

"You two are trouble," the Gray Man growled as the boys sat down. "I had to pull about fifteen kinds of rank on that police inspector investigating your case, and you turn around and do this." He turned away, buckling his seat belt as the takeoff announcement came.

Frank and Joe settled into their seats. But as he sat down Frank noticed that the old man was still on the plane, in the seat beside Martha.

Why did that guy lie about getting off the plane? Frank wondered. Then he stiffened as a thought hit him. He was never searched for weapons. He could be carrying anything!

# Chapter

## 7

THE JET'S ENGINES worked their way from a high-pitched whine to a dull rumble.

"Hey, c'mon," Joe said, breaking into Frank's thoughts. "Buckle up. We're almost on the runway." He hunched his shoulders in annoyance. "I don't know why you stuck me in the middle seat."

The Gray Man glared at him. "I was here first, and I didn't invite you. That's why I get the window seat."

"And I'm the older brother," Frank said, clicking his seat belt together. "That's why I get the seat on the aisle."

"I had to ask," Joe grumbled.

"I'll ask *you* something." Frank lowered his voice, staring suspiciously toward the front of the cabin. "Notice anybody else on the plane?"

47

"The old lady?" Joe said, leaning back as the plane began taxiing down the runway.

"The old guy is with her."

Joe stiffened. "He was supposed to get off," he whispered.

Frank nodded. "That's why I want the aisle seat."

The force of the plane's takeoff pushed the Hardy boys back in their seats. "It's probably just a coincidence or some kind of misunderstanding," Joe insisted in a whisper.

"Yeah." But Frank kept his eyes on the cockpit door—and on the seats right in front of it.

The takeoff was routine, and soon they were at cruising altitude high above the Atlantic. Over the intercom came the voice of a stewardess. "Passengers may now leave their seats if they desire."

The first passenger out of his seat was Martha's elderly friend. He shuffled back to the restroom with an embarrassed smile.

Joe saw that while Frank seemed to take no notice of the man, his fingers were on the buckle of his seat belt, ready to release himself in an instant if necessary.

"I think you're getting a little paranoid over all this business," Joe whispered after the man had entered the lavatory. "The poor guy's just going to the john. Do you really think that old geezer and his lady friend are going to try anything? You must be crazy."

The door to the restroom swung open with a bang. Standing in the doorway was the old man, but somehow he'd washed sixty years off his face. His clothes hung baggily around him. Joe gasped. In the man's left hand was an aerosol can—Mace. But gripped in his right was a hand grenade. At least he hasn't pulled the firing pin, Joe thought.

"Stay in your seats, and no one gets hurt!" the man commanded as he ran up the aisle. Too late, Joe realized that he spoke with a slight but detectable accent. "We're taking control of this plane in the name of the Assassins."

Frank burst from his seat, snapping a karate blow at the hijacker. It connected with his right wrist, paralyzing the hand. The grenade flew from nerveless fingers.

But the hijacker's other hand was operating fine. It sent a spray of Mace into Frank's face. The acrid stench of the chemical filled the air as Frank involuntarily backed away. He was choking and reeled in sudden blindness.

"Now you pay." The hijacker's voice was venomous as he prepared to club the helpless Frank.

But Joe had snapped open his seat belt. He barreled out of his row and crashed into the guy. They staggered across the aisle, crashing against the seat on the other side. Joe's hand clamped over the top of the spray can. He didn't want the Mace in *his* face.

He could hear sputtering sounds from the spray

nozzle as the contents of the can squirted into the palm of his hand. Even there, the chemicals burned his skin. Still worse, they made his hand slippery. He was losing his grip!

The hijacker twisted Joe's hand—and the can—free. Joe had just one move to make. Bracing one foot behind the man's ankle, he propelled them both into the laps of the people on the seat. At the same moment, he shoved his own chemical-covered hand straight into the terrorist's eyes.

The man tried to raise the spray can again, but the people in the seats had overcome their surprise and grabbed the man's arms. Still, he was able to release a cloud of the chemical as he thrashed about wildly.

But the Mace worked against him, too, as Joe kept his soaked hand over the man's face. The hijacker bucked and tore his face free, which was the opening Joe had been waiting for. As soon as the man had blindly twisted out of his grip, Joe's other hand drew back, cocked in a fist, and homed in for the point of the guy's jaw.

Frank, meanwhile, couldn't tell what was happening. He stumbled along the aisle, coughing. Tears ran down his cheeks, the effects of the chemical sprayed into his eyes. His brother's battle was a painful blur—until he felt a body brush past him.

Struggling to focus his half-blinded eyes, he caught a glimpse of gaily patterned cloth—the same pattern as the dress old Martha was wearing. But she had become amazingly spry as she pushed him aside and dived for an object on the floor. The grenade!

Frank lunged over her, blindly kicking out with his foot. His toe hit something solid, sending the grenade skittering along the floor.

The woman whirled on Frank, hissing something in a language he couldn't understand. She fumbled for a second with the large pin on her blouse. Frank squinted. No, it was too long to be a pin. It was more like the blade of a stiletto.

She slashed at Frank, who drew back and stumbled into the Gray Man, who'd also risen from his seat.

Before Frank and the Gray Man could disentangle themselves, the female terrorist had rushed down the aisle and grabbed the stewardess, who was trying to pick up the grenade.

The stewardess had been on her knees. The terrorist grabbed her by the hair and held the knife to her throat. "Nobody moves," the terrorist said, a smirk on her face, "or this one dies." She looked down at the grenade in the stewardess's hand. "Hand that up slowly. And do nothing foolish."

Frank stood frozen. Once the grenade was in the woman's hands, they'd all be dead.

"Wait a second." The voice came from behind him. "I'm an American official. If you want a hostage, I volunteer. Let the stewardess go." It was the Gray Man. He held his hands out to show that they were empty and pushed past Frank, masking him.

The female hijacker hesitated, stepping forward slightly, glancing at the distraction. Frank realized he'd never have a better chance. He launched a flying kick, past the Gray Man's side, past the stewardess's ear—right to the pit of the female terrorist's stomach.

The woman folded in the middle. At the same time, the Gray Man swept his arm out, pushing the stewardess away. Then Frank lashed his foot out again in a high kick. It connected with the female terrorist, and she flew down the aisle, landing flat on her back, the knife flashing just inches from the stewardess's face.

The Gray Man moved fast. One foot landed on the blade of the knife; the other kicked the woman's hand away.

Joe Hardy was hauling the unconscious male terrorist out of the seat where they'd fallen. The man hung limply in Joe's arms. The dangerous spray can rolled into the aisle. Frank stood blinking, still trying to work the chemical out of his eyes.

The Gray Man ripped off his tie and knelt by the stunned female hijacker, binding her hands. Suddenly he let go with one hand and reached for her jaw, but she twisted her head away. He grabbed her again, wedging her mouth open. "Too late!" he said, frustrated.

The woman's breathing became labored. Her body began jerking uncontrollably in convulsions. By the time Frank and Joe had rushed over, the woman had fallen back, suddenly still, her lips already turning blue.

A new scent filled the air. It was the smell of almonds, bitter almonds. "A cyanide capsule," the Gray Man exclaimed. "She's poisoned herself!"

# Chapter

## 8

A SHOCKED SILENCE hung over the plane for the rest of the trip across the Atlantic. The loudest things Frank and Joe heard were nervous murmurs among the passengers. Some wanted to return to the airport, but the Gray Man vetoed that, virtually commandeering the plane with his government authority.

The grenade had been locked away, and crew members gently removed the female terrorist from the cabin. The male hijacker sat in the first seat again, tied up and gagged. The Gray Man had checked out his mouth and carefully removed the cyanide capsule that was hidden in a false tooth.

After that, the Gray Man spent most of the flight up in the cockpit. He emerged only after the plane landed. "Come on." He beckoned to the Hardys.

Stepping into the cockpit, Frank and Joe found

the plane doors open, a ladder reaching up to them.

"You know, I expected better accommodations at Heathrow," Frank said.

"This doesn't look like the London airport," Joe added, peering out the door, "unless they knocked down the arrival buildings and moved a bunch of Harrier jets in."

Frank looked out at a squadron of fighter planes lined up on the tarmac.

"It's an RAF base near Portsmouth," the Gray Man explained. "Now if you'll kindly get down that ladder, you'll be out of the way of those military policemen who are waiting to come aboard."

Frank and Joe stared down at the airmen clustered around the ladder. They wore white armbands and carried pistols. "What are the military police doing here?" Joe asked.

"The MPs? Two jobs. One, they're collecting our tied-up friend for delivery to British Intelligence. Two, they're keeping everyone else aboard the plane."

"Why?"

"To keep our arrival secret. We know the Assassins arranged this hijacking. But all they'll know is that the whole plane has disappeared—probably on its way to Libya," the Gray Man explained with a grim smile. "They won't know we're here in England. Maybe it will give us the advantage of surprise."

"But the people on the plane—"

"Will stay there, until the operation is finished." The Gray Man gestured to the ladder. "Now get down there. We have a helicopter waiting to take us and our friend the hijacker to London."

In the distance, an army copter dropped lightly to the concrete runway, its rotors idling. Frank and Joe clambered down the ladder, followed by the Gray Man. Then the MPs climbed up, and soon the hijacker was being lowered to the ground in a sling.

With the Hardys supporting the bound captive on each side, they followed the Gray Man to the copter.

"Perkins!" the Gray Man said when he saw the pilot. "I didn't think you'd been demoted to chauffeur."

The pilot, who had a round, pink face and a silly grin, looked like a dopey young English lord from an old movie. "My pilot's license is approved for helis. And Sir Nigel wanted absolute security on this trip."

"Orders from the very top, eh?" The Gray Man returned the grin. "Boys, let me introduce Edwin Perkins. Don't let that dumb smile fool you. He's chief aide to Sir Nigel Folliott, head of British Intelligence. Perkins, Frank and Joe Hardy."

"You aren't introducing your silent friend over there?" Perkins nodded to the bound hijacker.

"He wouldn't talk even if the gag were out of his mouth," the Gray Man replied.

"Probably not, if he's what you say he is," Perkins said as the copter lifted off. "It's very rare to get your hands on an Assassin—alive, that is."

As if to prove Perkins's words, their captive made a lunge for the door as the helicopter leveled off fifty feet from the ground.

"What the—!" Joe grabbed the guy before he could plunge through the door.

"He's really trying to kill himself," Frank said quietly.

"So how do we make him talk?" Joe whispered back.

After the helicopter landed at the secret British Intelligence center, that was exactly the problem facing the interrogation experts. "What's your name then, mate?" one of them asked.

The prisoner stared in stony silence. With his old-man makeup completely off, he looked hardly older than the Hardys.

"He might as well still be wearing the gag," Joe said.

They watched as the interrogators played "Good Cop/Bad Cop." The one who spoke first was friendly and fair. The other was hostile and scary.

"How's it going? Any way I can make it easier for you?" the Good Cop said.

"You can take these off." The prisoner gestured at the heavy manacles that held him in his chair.

"Those are for your own good. We've seen what you've tried to do." The Good Cop shook his head. "I was thinking more along the lines of something to drink."

"Forget it," the Bad Cop cut in. "We're not here to coddle this scum." He pulled a sheet of paper from his pocket. "I've got a list of questions here, and I expect to get them all answered."

The questioning went on and on, with no effect, not even when the Bad Cop started roughing up the terrorist. The prisoner actually laughed. "You think I do not know this game?" His laughter grew louder. "Assassins do not tell secrets."

He nodded toward the Hardys. "Maybe your game would work on those two. They are just boys."

"We were good enough to capture you," Joe said.

"Oh, yes, the great fighter." The prisoner's smile was mocking as he looked at Joe. "Did losing that girl make you fight harder?"

Joe's face went pale and hard. "You know about that?"

"Oh, I did not have anything to do with it," the prisoner said, watching the muscles in Joe's neck tighten. "Except, of course, to work with the bomb—"

Before anyone could move, Joe was in midair,

leaping at the prisoner. The chair and the bound man fell to the floor as Joe smashed into them, locking his hands around the terrorist's throat.

"Joe, stop it." Frank tried to pull his brother free, but he couldn't break Joe's choke-hold. The two burly interrogators and Perkins had to step in as well. Finally, the prisoner lay gasping on one side of the room. Joe struggled in the interrogators' grasp on the other side. There was no light of reason in his eyes, and his face was murderous.

"This guy was playing you," Frank shouted into Joe's face. "He can't kill himself, so he's got to get himself killed. That's why he worked on you."

Joe stopped trying to break free. "So he's alive," he growled at last. "He still hasn't said anything."

"Ah, but I think that will change now. I've been waiting for our expert to arrive. And here he is," Perkins said as the door to the interrogation room swung open.

In walked a short, bald man with a plump, shiny face. His watery blue eyes darted nervously around the room from behind the thick lenses of his glasses. "I-is it all right to come in?" he asked.

"*This* is your expert interrogator?" Joe stared in disbelief.

"Thanks to the miracle of modern chemistry, yes," said Perkins. "Go on, Fosby."

The little man opened the case he was carrying and loaded a hypodermic needle. Then he crossed the room to Joe and the two interrogators. "Hold him firmly now."

"Not him," Perkins said. "The chap on the floor."

As soon as the terrorist saw the needle, he pulled himself upright and rushed for the door. He didn't get far. The interrogators were waiting. In five seconds he was back on the floor in a hammerlock, his sleeve rolled up. Moments later, the injection was beginning to work.

"This is one of our better truth serums," Perkins said, watching as a dreamy look came over the prisoner's face.

Fosby was talking to him in a gentle voice. "What's your name, son?"

The prisoner slurred words for a second or two, then said, "Hassan."

"I want you to tell me some things, Hassan. You'll do that for me, won't you?"

"I . . . tell . . ."

"I want to know about the London safe house," said Fosby. Frank and Joe glanced at each other. So the Assassins had a hideout in town!

"The safe house," Fosby repeated. "I want the code words to get in. You know them, don't you?"

Hassan's face went tight as he heard the words "safe house." At the mention of "code words," he began to shake and twitch. His eyes opened wide with horror as he screamed something in a foreign language.

Fosby's voice grew sharp. "Forget that. Forget it. Rest . . ." He looked over at Perkins. "Sorry, sir. He's been conditioned against giving that information away. If I press, he'll just go into a fit like that and die."

Fosby paused and rubbed a hand over his shiny scalp. "Standard procedure among the Assassins. All of them undergo the conditioning from time to time. Helps them keep everything secret."

Perkins's face was thoughtful. "We'll have to work our way back to the last conditioning session then. Start with his last mission."

"Hassan," Fosby said gently, "tell me about the hijacking."

"Rush job." Hassan sighed. "Four of us to go for American operation. We hardly arrive, when Selim and Rashid are sent off. Then Leila and I are ordered to get on plane. Almost no time to get tickets."

"And the disguises?" Fosby asked.

"They were ready—and the wheelchair. It is a standard way to board planes."

"You say it was a rush job?"

"We were given the description of a man.

Eliminate him and anyone with him," Hassan said. "Destroy entire plane if necessary."

Joe looked at the Gray Man. "You're famous," he whispered.

"Afraid we would miss the plane," Hassan went on.

"How did they know?" Frank whispered.

"Shhh." Joe wanted to hear the next question.

"Who gave the order?"

Hassan began to sweat. "A voice on the phone. He gave us orders only that once."

"Hassan, you know his name." Fosby was leaning forward, eyes sharp.

"I—am not . . ." The twitching was back now.

"Hassan, you know who it was."

"Cannot." Hassan's arms began to jerk against his manacles.

"We're getting close to his conditioning," Fosby said. "Hassan," his voice prodded. "His code name."

The prisoner's eyes were bugging out of his head. His face was red and strained as he almost gobbled the words. ". . . taken over American operation. Very important . . ."

"Important?" Fosby echoed.

"Important mission," Hassan said.

"What mission?"

"Don't know. *Don't know!*" The words were almost a scream.

"Who? Who is it, Hassan? Who's running the mission?" Fosby asked.

It looked as if the fit would tear the prisoner apart. Finally, he wailed an answer, "Al-Rousasa," and collapsed.

That name seemed to mean something to the intelligence people in the room. Frank and Joe saw the Gray Man's eyes light in recognition.

"Who's this Al-Rousasa character?" Joe wanted to know.

"A very heavy hitter on the international terrorism scene." The Gray Man frowned. "He may be the one who set the bomb in your car. But if he's involved, there's something much bigger going on in Bayport."

"Al-Rousasa." Frank repeated the name. "What is that? Arabic?"

"It's a code name," the Gray Man said. "Literally translated, it means 'The Bullet.' " His face was very grim. "And they say that whenever the Bullet is aimed, the target is dead."

# Chapter

## 9

FRANK AND JOE watched in silence as the interrogator knelt by the captive. "We'll get no more from him now," Fosby said. "Not for a long time—if ever."

"Well, we know nothing more about the safe house," Perkins said, "and if we believe our sources, half of the Assassins' leadership council is in there right now."

"Then we should get moving, before they get suspicious about the hijacking." The Gray Man turned to the Hardys. "Let's get you some gear."

Soon, the Hardys were in an empty office, changing into comfortable black jeans and black zippered jackets. "This stuff looks like it's easy to move in, at least," said Joe.

"Wait till you try this on," said Frank, pulling

his jacket over the bulk of a bulletproof vest. "It's like wearing a life jacket for underwear." He zipped up the jacket, then turned the handle on the door. It didn't open.

"What the—?" he said, straining, but the handle didn't turn.

Joe joined him, twisting the handle, pulling it, but it didn't budge. "Hey!" he shouted, banging his fist on the door.

A shadow appeared on the reinforced pebble-glass window in the door. Though they couldn't see the face, both Hardys recognized who it was—the Gray Man.

"We'll just keep you here during the raid," the government man said. "You'll be safe and sound, and out of the way of stray bullets."

"Wait a minute!" shouted Frank, but the Gray Man had already headed down the corridor.

The boys looked around their temporary prison, an eight-by-eight-foot office with a desk piled high with papers, two chairs, and no windows. In two steps, Joe was at the desk, grabbing a paperweight from one of the piles. "This looks like our ticket out of here," he said, winding up. With the speed of his best fastball, the paperweight smashed into the window on the door.

And bounced off.

Joe stared in shock for a second, then recovered the paperweight from the floor. Holding it in his hand, he hammered at the window. He might as well have been tickling it with a flower.

"I need something heavier," Joe said. Tossing the paperweight away, he took one of the chairs and swung it at the window. The chair bounced off, too. "What *is* this stuff?"

Frank climbed onto the other chair, examining the ceiling.

"Get real, Frank. We'd never fit through the air-system vent."

"I guess you're right. Keep working on the window," Frank said, mouthing the word "bugs." Joe resumed pounding away at the door as Frank moved his chair over to the wall, testing the ceiling tiles with his fingers. Finally, as Joe hit the door extra hard, Frank formed a fist and rammed the tile out of its framework.

Peering into the musty darkness, he smiled. The walls extended only to a hung ceiling, leaving a foot-high passage into the next office!

"You might as well put the chair down and sit on it, Joe," Frank said for the benefit of any unseen listeners. "We're never going to get out of here." He beckoned Joe over, then worked more tiles loose.

Frank climbed into the airspace with a hand from Joe. Balancing himself on the wall (the tiles were too light to support his weight), Frank listened for any sounds from the office next door. Nothing.

But just as he was about to pry up one of the tiles, Frank heard coughing. Someone was in there!

Frank slipped back through the hole, shaking his head to Joe. They moved the chair to the opposite wall, and while Joe whistled loudly, Frank dislodged more tiles. Leaning into the airspace again, he held his breath. If someone was in *this* office, they were stuck.

But the office remained silent, even when Frank cautiously levered up a ceiling tile. Frank looked down through the opening and saw an empty desk. He quickly worked to enlarge the hole, then crawled through. When Joe joined him seconds later, Frank was already at the door, trying the handle.

It turned without a problem.

Easing the door open, Frank and Joe scanned the corridor. Their eyes darted around, sensitive to the slightest movement. No one was there.

They walked down the corridor, pausing at each intersection, checking out their surroundings before moving.

Joe brought them to a halt when he heard low conversation not far away. The boys looked around a corner and saw a garage filled with a dozen men dressed in the same black clothes the Hardys wore but carrying Sterling submachine guns.

The Gray Man and Edwin Perkins entered through another doorway. Perkins was slipping a pistol into his holster. "Sergeant Morris," he called to a gray-haired veteran, "let's get this show on the road."

"All right," roared the sergeant. "Into the lorry!"

The troops started clambering inside a large, battered panel truck, and the garage door rose with a metallic clatter.

"They're leaving," Frank whispered when all the men were aboard.

"Not without us!" Joe responded.

The truck's engine roared to life. Joe sprinted across the garage, leaping onto the rear bumper and wrapping his arm around a pole at the back of the truck. He waved his arm in a silent "Come on!" to Frank. Shaking his head in amazement, Frank grasped a metal projection on the other side just as the truck lurched into motion.

The ride through South London was short. Even so, the Hardys were nearly thrown off several times as the truck jounced over badly paved streets.

The neighborhoods of red brick houses that the truck passed through became seedier and poorer. Frank and Joe saw many stores that had been boarded up. They noticed that signs were written in Arabic letters—Pakistani.

Frank knew that people from all over the old British Empire—from the West Indies, Africa, and Asia—had come to the neighborhood of Brixton. And they'd stayed there. He even saw burned buildings, leftovers from riots. It was easy to see that the Assassins knew what they were doing when they picked Brixton for their safe house.

The truck bounced heavily as it turned onto a cobblestoned street with many of the cobblestones missing or broken. Most of the houses on the dead-end street were just shells, but one dingy three-story building still showed signs of life. At least curtains were flapping in the windows.

Down the block, a group of city construction workers struggled to repair a broken streetlamp. And at the corner a gang of Pakistani workmen tried to renovate a burned-out shop. The only other car on the street was a Post Office van. The mailman was just climbing out.

But everything changed as the truck rolled to a stop right in front of the safe house. The shop windows turned into clouds of tinkling glass shards as the workmen inside—Gurkhas, Nepalese soldiers who joined the British Army—let loose with machine guns. Their covering fire tore into the windows of the upper floors of the safe house.

Machine guns were snatched out of the "construction workers'" toolboxes, too. Even the "mailman" whipped a Sterling from his sack, hosing the ground-floor windows with bullets.

The doors of the lorry flew open, and the attack force pelted out to add to the fire. When the Gray Man saw the unexpected hitchhikers, he froze, pistol in hand, his eyes bulging. "What the—get *down,* you idiots!"

He leaped to the ground, pulling the Hardys into the cover of the truck. All around them bullets still flew.

Six men rushed up the front stairs of the safe house with a battering ram, swinging it back even as they ran. The ram smashed into the door, bounced back, and was swung forward again—and again. With practiced rhythm, the team kept slamming away.

Finally, the hinges began to give. With a grinding noise, the door cracked, then sagged. The team hurled the ram forward, sending the door crashing in. Unslinging their guns, they covered the front hall of the house. "Nothing moving, sir," the sergeant in charge called as Perkins and his team ran up the stairs.

"No response to our fire, either," Perkins said, peering inside. "Let's go in."

Pistols and machine guns poised, they entered the hallway.

The covering fire stopped, as everyone waited tensely to hear what was in store for the raiding team. The minutes straggled by, but the street remained silent.

"Getting right spooky, it is," one of the covering gunners muttered.

From inside the house came the sounds of doors being kicked in. Occasionally, one of the raiders would appear at a window, waving an "all clear." Once, a couple of shots rang out, but the sergeant shouted, "False alarm."

Finally, Perkins appeared in the wrecked doorway, his pistol holstered and a frustrated frown on his face. "No one's there!" he said.

The Gray Man headed up the stairs. "Could they be on the roof?" he called.

"Not unless they flew," Perkins replied as Frank and Joe joined them. "There was enough dust on the top floors to grow crops." He stared at the Hardys for a moment. "And what are these two doing here?"

The Gray Man smiled without mirth. "Well, they've arrived just in time for the search."

Since the all clear had been given, the house filled with searchers, from the top to the ground floors. Using plans picked up from the Hall of Records, they even checked for secret passages in the walls.

"This is ridiculous," Perkins groused as they headed down into the cellar of the building. "They can't have disappeared. Our people have seen Assassins going in. They've spotted leaders here. And we've had the building surrounded."

"No windows or anything overlooked?" the Gray Man asked.

"We worked from those plans," Perkins replied testily. "There's no way in or out that wasn't guarded."

"I guess that means they're down here, then." The Gray Man shone his flashlight around the cellar. At one time partitions had been up, but the makeshift walls had all come down. In one corner, they saw the remains of the coal cellar. In another, some crates apparently had been disassembled. Perkins looked at the piles of wood.

"Some of these have armory markings," he said, his voice going hard. "Stolen weapons, probably."

"Looks like they were storing lots of things here," Frank said.

"The question is, how?" said Joe. "And where?"

"Well, the answer may be over here." The Gray Man had been shining his flashlight along the floor. He stopped it in another corner of the cellar. Set in the concrete floor was a heavy wooden trapdoor.

"It certainly does explain everything," the Gray Man said. "My nose told me about it since we were on the stairs. Didn't you catch the earthy smell down here? Turned earth, as if someone had been digging. I'll bet that little addition won't appear on any of your official plans," he said to Perkins.

Perkins stared. "You're saying that they dug an escape tunnel?"

The Gray Man nodded. "A lot of work, but it paid off for them, didn't it?" He knelt by the trapdoor. "This could lead just next door, or to another building entirely. Or they could have cut into the sewer system."

"Wherever it leads, I'm sure it's far from here," Perkins said gloomily.

"There's only one way to find out." The Gray Man reached down and grabbed the ring-pull on the trapdoor.

Something clicked in Frank Hardy's mind, something about the way the Assassins worked. Unconsciously, he'd been expecting it ever since they'd come into the building. But there'd been nothing—

"Wait a second!" he yelled, running forward. "These guys love bombs! It could be booby—"

The Gray Man had already heaved the door up. He and Frank disappeared in the flash of an explosion!

# Chapter

## 10

THE BLAST OF the demolition charges threw Joe Hardy and Perkins to the floor. Immediately, they scrambled to their feet and ran to the two still figures lying by the wrecked trapdoor. "Frank," Joe managed to choke out, "Not Frank, too."

But as he reached his brother, Frank began to stir, pushing himself up on one arm. "The door shielded me from the worst of the blast. But him—" he mumbled, looking toward the Gray Man. "Was I able to push him far enough away?"

Perkins knelt by the fallen agent, looking very different from the aristocratic pilot Frank and Joe had met at the airfield. His face was covered with dirt, and the beginnings of a bruise showed on his cheek. His expression was serious as he checked for a pulse. "He's still breathing," he said. "Which he wouldn't be if you hadn't pushed him away. But . . ." He shook his head. "He's very bad."

"Mr. Perkins!" Sergeant Morris and a private came down the stairs. "Are you all right? The whole house feels like it's going to go!"

From the ceiling overhead came ominous creaking and groaning sounds. The foundation of the century-old house had been severely shaken.

"We've got to get out!" Joe's voice cut over the noises. "Give us a hand here!"

He helped Frank to his feet as the two soldiers helped Perkins gently pick up the Gray Man. "Up the stairs—hurry!" Perkins shouted.

The creaking in the ceiling became a horrible grinding noise. "Some of the beams must have cracked," Frank muttered as they stumbled up the stairs. Just as they reached the doorway a big section of the first floor sagged, then crashed into the basement, right onto the spot where they'd been standing seconds before.

The entire house then began to sway and to crumple inward. Dozens of hands grabbed Frank and Joe, hustling them away. More helped to move the injured Gray Man.

Frank and Joe stood at the entrance to the dead-end street, watching as the old brick building collapsed completely.

"I'll tell you one thing," Joe said quietly as the roof fell in.

"What?" asked Frank.

"They'll never call *that* a safe house again."

By then, fire engines and emergency personnel were arriving. Tender hands bundled the Gray Man aboard an ambulance. "You're coming along, too," said Perkins, leading Frank and Joe to the medical people.

Doctors at the hospital declared that Frank was merely shaken up. They were much more grim about the Gray Man's condition and immediately wheeled him into surgery. "Come on," said Perkins when he found the Hardys pacing around the waiting room.

"What now?" asked Frank.

"I'd say it was time for you two to wash up and get some fresh clothes and maybe some rest. Then perhaps we should get you in to talk with the Chief."

"The Chief" turned out to be Sir Nigel Folliott, head of British Intelligence. Hollywood couldn't have gotten a better actor for the part. Folliott was a man with a mane of ginger hair going silver, and large, handsome features. As Perkins ushered the Hardys into his huge wood-paneled, book-lined office, Sir Nigel rose from his old-fashioned teak desk.

"I've been getting regular reports from the hospital on our friend," he said after introductions had been made. "He's remarkably fit for such a nondescript-looking sort. The doctors say he'll pull through."

Joe and Frank smiled at that.

"However," Sir Nigel went on, "he'll be in

hospital for some time. And he's still not conscious. I understand you joined his investigation"—he coughed—"rather informally. So the question is, what do I do with you?"

"Well, Sir Nigel, we have some questions," Frank said. "We came here after the Assassins. Have any more been caught?"

"Frankly, no," Sir Nigel said. "We found the tunnel they used. Hard to miss, actually. They used too much explosive to seal off the digging and blew out one of the nearby roads. Blasted thing went three blocks to an abandoned building. Well outside the cordon we'd drawn up."

"So they got away," Joe said, disappointed.

"From that building, yes. From London . . . well, that's another story. We've sealed the city. Buses, motorways, airports, even the shipping routes are being watched."

"You're saying it's impossible for them to escape?" Frank asked.

Sir Nigel shook his head. "Not impossible—but very dangerous. If they want to escape arrest, they'll have to lie low for the time being."

"That means they won't be able to have much to do with whatever is going on in Bayport," Frank said. "I suppose that's a win."

"And you've already cost Al-Rousasa the reinforcements he was expecting—that pair who tried to hijack your plane," Perkins pointed out. "That's a victory, too."

He smiled. "In case you're wondering, the

people who were on the flight with you are now arriving in London—a little stiff from having to sit around in the plane so long, but otherwise safe and sound."

"The surviving hijacker can't tell us anything more about the planned terror campaign in the U.S.," Sir Nigel said. "We've passed everything we found on to your government.

"But the question still remains—what about you?" His face grew serious as he went on. "Perkins told me a bit about your backgrounds and why you've involved yourselves in this case. I tell you frankly, I don't approve of people with personal axes to grind."

"So what do you figure on doing?" Joe cut in. "Do you want to keep us here?" His scowl clearly showed what he thought of that idea.

"Sir Nigel," Frank said more diplomatically, "if you've informed the American authorities of what's going on, maybe you should send us back to Bayport so that we can"—he paused for a second—"give whatever assistance we can."

"What are you talking about? 'Give whatever assistance we can'?" Joe burst out. "I want to kill—"

A look from Frank silenced him.

"Um, I mean, I really want to see this Al-Rousasa caught," Joe said. "And if there's anything I can do to help—"

"We do know the town," Frank put in.

78

Sir Nigel gazed at them seriously. "Under the Official Secrets Act, I'd be quite within my rights to keep you. But under the circumstances, I'll accept your promise to tell no one—*no one*—about what took place after you left Bayport."

He smiled suddenly. "I can see that you both feel strongly about getting home. And that was Perkins's suggestion as well."

He picked up an envelope from his desk. "These tickets are for the next flight. Somehow, I suspected you'd want to be on it."

Frank took the tickets gratefully. "You're right, Sir Nigel. Thank you."

Perkins was just opening the door for them when they heard a disturbance in the outer office.

"I demand to see Sir Nigel!" a voice cried angrily. "That collapsed building was a safe house for the Assassins, and I want to know—"

Frank recognized the voice and quickly shut the door.

"That's *Dad*," Joe whispered. "What do we do now?"

"Sir Nigel," Frank said, "I think we have a problem." Quickly he explained Fenton Hardy's arrangements for them and where they were supposed to be. "So if our father finds us here, we'll give away the whole show."

"Well, you are heading home now," Sir Nigel said with a conspiratorial smile. "Perkins, why don't you go out there and talk to Mr. Hardy? In the meantime, I'll show the boys the other exit from the office."

On the flight home, the Hardys talked quietly about their narrow escape.

"If Dad had seen us coming out of that office, he'd have skinned us alive," Joe said.

Frank nodded. "It's just lucky that we heard him before he saw us."

"He didn't seem happy," Joe went on. "Maybe his investigation isn't coming along too well."

"No better than ours, I guess." Frank closed his eyes and leaned back in his seat.

"Well, Dad's got a tighter schedule than we have, Frank. He can't stay undercover forever. There's that big Walker rally at the mall. He's the head of security. He'll have to be there."

Frank's eyes snapped open. "What idiots we've been," he said, breathing hard.

"What?" Joe said.

"A bombing at the mall. What connection does it have to Iola? Why was she at the mall?" Frank turned to his brother, who was staring at him doubtfully.

"Joe, what do we know about this Al-Rousasa?"

"He's an Assassin. A heavy hitter. Never misses."

"Besides that," Frank said. "Remember what that guy we caught told us."

Joe pulled his brows together as he thought.

"He was supposed to be in America to run a big terror campaign."

"And?" Frank prompted.

"And what?"

"That campaign had its timing thrown off by a special job." Frank shook his head. "Don't you see?"

"See what?"

"Iola—all of us—were at the mall for a dress rehearsal of Philip Walker's appearance this Saturday. Suppose that bomb in our car was a dress rehearsal, too. *Suppose Al-Rousasa was practicing how he'd assassinate Philip Walker!*"

# Chapter

## 11

FRANK HARDY'S FIRST question on landing at the airport was, "Where's the phone?"

Joe stared in surprise. "Phone? I thought we were going to get right in the car and . . . Oh."

"Right," Frank said. "No car."

Joe jingled the change in his pockets. "And not enough money for a cab."

Frank led the way to a pay phone. "I'm going to see if I can get hold of Callie. She'll give us a lift. And then our first stop is the police station."

Frank made the call; then he and Joe waited for Callie. Frank looked impatiently at his watch until Callie's green Nova finally pulled up. "Frank! Joe!" she called. "Where have you guys been? I've been trying to call—"

Frank gave her a quick kiss. "I can't explain right now, but we've got to get to the police station."

Callie's dark eyes narrowed in concern when she heard their destination. "We're going to be cutting it mighty close," she said as they got in. "The day shift ends right now."

The street in front of the station was jammed with patrol cars. "Looks like the changing of the guard," Frank said as Callie pulled up at the corner.

He and Joe piled out. "Let's just hope the people we've got to see haven't left yet."

They ran through the big double doors and across the corridor to the desk officer. "Excuse me," Frank said. "I'd like to talk to whoever is handling the security for Saturday's rally at the mall."

The man behind the desk was a stranger. "Look, boys, right now isn't the best time—"

Behind him a door opened, and Con Riley stepped out, dressed in street clothes. "Hi, boys," he said when he noticed Frank and Joe. Seeing the frustrated look on their faces, he turned to the man behind the desk. "Aw, stop giving them a hard time, Jerry. I know these guys."

"They want to see the man in charge of security for the mall rally," Jerry told Con.

"Oh. I'll take 'em." Con's face was unreadable as he led the Hardys into the Detective Division—and over to the door marked S. BUTLER.

"Oh, no," Joe moaned.

"*He's* in charge of security?" Frank said.

"Well, it's his specialty," Con replied. "He ran the detail that guarded the United Nations in New York." He rushed on. "He's a tough cop, but a good one. He—"

"Does anyone here like him?" Joe asked.

"He's a good cop—" Riley began again.

"That's not what I asked." Joe looked Con in the eye.

Con looked back. "No," he answered finally. "Most of us think he's a real pain in the—"

The door opened, and Butler stepped out. "What's all the noise out here?" He stopped when he saw Frank and Joe. "Oh. It's *you* two. Have a nice vacation, boys?" Although his poker face was still in place, Butler's voice dripped sarcasm.

"Inspector, we've got to talk with you." Frank stepped forward. Con Riley instantly took the opportunity to fade back.

"I can't tell you how honored I am that you decided to drop by," Butler said, cutting Frank off. His shook his finger, nearly jabbing Frank's face. "I told you not to leave town. And what's the first thing you do? Pull strings and disappear. Maybe some of the dumb hicks around here will take that, but not a *real* cop."

Butler grabbed Frank by the arm and pulled him into his office. "You too, bright eyes," he said to Joe.

Frank spun out of Butler's grip as soon as they were in the office. "Inspector, you're running security for the rally on Saturday. We think some-one's going to try to kill Philip Walker there."

"Oh, you do?" Butler's tone was frankly mocking. "Do you know who?"

"An international terrorist organization called the Assassins. They've sent one of their best men, Al-Rousasa, over here to run a series of terror attacks in American cities. But he was switched to a special project—right after Philip Walker began talking about fighting terrorists." Frank looked at Butler, who had walked to his desk and leaned against it.

The inspector's arms were crossed over his chest, and his face gave nothing away. Trying to convince that expressionless face was the hardest thing Frank had ever done.

"This rally at the mall is a big thing for Walker's campaign. There'll be lots of media coverage, and lots of his supporters will be there. But it will also be the perfect event for a terrorist. I'm certain that Al-Rousasa is aiming for it.

"Look at how many supplies have disappeared from the mall recently," Frank went on as he showed Butler the list in his notebook. "I think the bombing of our car was just preparation for what will happen on Saturday."

Butler still didn't move. "And what do you expect me to do?"

"Search the mall," Joe put in eagerly. "We can still move before the terrorist does."

"Let me get this straight," Butler said, pacing

in front of them. "You think this guy blew up your girlfriend so he could get in a little practice on killing Philip Walker? That's how he's going to spend his Saturday?

"Now," he went on, "what I should do is get every cop in town to turn the mall upside down before the big rally. I've got just one question. Do you think this terrorist might escape on a UFO?"

Butler whirled to face the Hardys, his expression becoming angry for a moment, then grimacing, then going masklike again. "How stupid do you think I am?" Butler shouted. "I knew you'd come up with some sort of cock-and-bull story to beat the rap on getting that girl killed. But this one wins the prize!"

"Inspector," Frank said, "we're telling you the truth."

"Oh, sure," Butler said. "You have any proof of this little fairy tale? Somebody to back you up? Evidence? Something a little better than a list in your notebook?"

"We—" Frank stopped. He couldn't reveal anything that had happened in London. He and Joe had made a promise to Sir Nigel. And there was no way the Gray Man could speak for them. "You could call—" Again he stopped. He could just imagine Butler's response to being told about British Intelligence.

"Well, you could talk to our father," Joe finally said.

"Oh, great. Are you sure Daddy will put in a good word for his darling boys? And where do I get in touch with the great Fenton Hardy? I've been trying to talk to him for days."

Joe bowed his head. "We—uh—don't know."

"That's really great, Sherlock." Butler turned his back on them. "Get out of here before I throw you out."

Once again, Frank and Joe found themselves storming out of Butler's office.

"Come on," said Frank, leading the way down a corridor. "We've got to go over this clown's head." But when they reached Chief Collig's office, the lights were out.

"Hey!" said a voice behind them. Jerry, the desk cop, came hurrying forward. "What do you two think you're doing?"

"We need to see Chief Collig," Joe said.

"Well, you'll see him tomorrow," the policeman replied. "He's left for the day."

"Great," Joe muttered as Jerry marched them outside.

Frank rushed over to the green Nova. "Callie," he asked, "did you see Chief Collig leave?"

"Yup," she replied. "Just a couple of minutes ago."

"Think you can catch up with him?" Frank asked as he and Joe climbed in.

"Let's find out." Callie hit the gas and pulled smoothly away from the curve.

The chief's route home took him away from downtown Bayport, along the Shore Road. As soon as they were out of traffic, Callie started speeding up. Far ahead, they saw a pair of taillights—taillights that grew rapidly nearer.

"It's a cop car," Callie said.

"It has to be the chief's," Joe agreed.

"Flash your lights at him," said Frank. "We've got to get his attention."

"The way we're speeding, I think we've got his attention," Callie said. Still, she flicked her headlight control.

The blinker on top of the police car began to revolve as it headed to the side of the road. "All right, pull over," said a voice over the car's loudspeaker.

When Frank and Joe got out of the car, they found the chief's chauffeur standing in the beams of Callie's headlights, his hand on his pistol butt. "Chief," Frank called out, "I've got to talk with you."

"What the—" Chief Ezra Collig stepped out. "Frank and Joe Hardy! What do you think you're doing, driving around like maniacs!"

"We had to catch up with you, Chief," Frank said.

"It's important," Joe added.

"Have you found out something about Iola Morton?" Collig asked.

"Yes. But it's even bigger," Frank said. He

explained about the Assassins and about his suspicions that the Walker rally could come under attack. "It would be a massacre," he finished. "We've got to search that mall."

Chief Collig's face was serious. "You won't like to hear this, boys," he said. "But I can understand why Butler reacted the way he did. You don't have any evidence." He shook his head helplessly. "You want me to put all my men on a time-consuming job just on your say-so."

"Chief—" said Joe.

"You've done a lot of good work, but you just don't know what you're asking this time." Chief Collig started walking back to his car. "If you had anyone to back you up—your father, for instance . . ."

"He probably won't arrive until Walker does, and then it will be too late," Frank said. "You've *got* to okay that search."

"I can't do that unless you can give me something more solid to go on." The chief climbed into his car. "Sorry, boys."

"We blew it!" Joe said as the chief's car roared off.

"I know, and I can hardly believe it." Joe had to strain to hear his brother's voice over the noise of the departing engine.

"We've got to convince them. But how?" Frank's murmuring was still almost inaudible under the engine noise—even though the chief's taillights were rapidly disappearing.

Something's not right, Joe thought, turning to Frank. At that second, in Callie's beams, he caught a silhouette. A dark sedan, lights out, was heading straight for them!

# Chapter

# 12

THE ONRUSHING CAR flashed in front of Callie Shaw's Nova, obviously aiming for Frank and Joe. But the Hardys weren't standing targets. They split up, heading for either shoulder of the road.

Tires squealed as the driver changed course. "Frank!" Callie screamed. The roar of the engine drowned out her words. Frank Hardy whirled to find the car almost on top of him, and no place to run. His muscles clenched for a dive he knew wouldn't take him far enough.

From the corner of his eye, he caught movement. Joe was sprinting across the road toward him, racing the car, throwing himself at Frank in a flying tackle. His extra momentum flung them out of danger even as the car swerved in a futile effort to nail them. The Hardys tumbled through the underbrush as the car roared down the road.

Frank untangled himself from Joe and staggered to his feet. "Get up! We still have a chance to catch him!"

Joe followed him to the road. "Callie! Start the car! We're going after him!"

They piled in and the Nova shot forward. "That guy was moving pretty fast," Joe said. "Do you think the Nova can catch him?"

"He's boxed in," Frank said. "Chief Collig is ahead of him, and we're behind. If he zooms past the chief's car—"

"Collig will go after him." Joe grinned. "I don't think the chief would enjoy someone trying to blow his doors off."

"And we're here to keep him from doubling back," Callie added.

"Right," said Frank. "We've got him—as long as there are no turnoffs. Does either of you know this stretch of road?"

"We have miles before we hit anything," Callie said. "It's pretty desolate around here. No roads, no houses, no driveways."

"There is one turnoff, though," Joe remarked. "A little bit ahead of here. It's a hill overlooking the river. Iola and I used to come—" He broke off whatever he was going to say.

"We, uh, know the place you mean," Callie said. "But you'd really have to live around here to know about it."

"And Al-Rousasa is a stranger to Bayport," Frank pointed out. "I think it's safe to go on."

Two seconds after passing the turnoff, they heard a car engine behind them. Joe swore between gritted teeth, staring out the rear windshield. The escaping car had no lights. Only the faintest traces of movement showed in the dark. "He *was* in there."

Callie sent the car in a wild U-turn, nearly spinning them out. She hit the gas, and the Nova sped back the way it had come. But the pursuit was hopeless. They never caught sight of the car.

Joe said nothing, just pounded his fist into the backseat over and over again. The silence grew thick.

"All right." Frank's voice was quiet. "We're back to square one. Anyone get a look at the car? The driver? The license plate?"

"Everything happened so quickly," Callie said. "I hardly had a chance."

"I was too busy rolling around with Frank." Joe turned to his brother. "If you want a good description of the third button on your shirt, I could give you that."

"Callie's lights were shining in my eyes." Frank shook his head. "All I saw was a silhouette of one person in the car."

"Al-Rousasa?" Joe said.

Frank shrugged. "If it was, I couldn't tell you anything except that his ears don't stick out. I didn't see any features."

"What do you mean, *'If* it was'?" Callie asked. "Who else would it have been?"

"Whoever tried to run us down followed us from the police station," Frank said. "There's no way he'd know we'd follow Chief Collig or that we'd stop here. This hit-and-run thing wasn't planned. But this guy used that turnoff—something nobody from out of town would know about."

"You're right," Callie said. "Every kid in town knows about this spot. It's a great place to go after a date."

"Except for the cops who shine flashlights in the window," Frank said.

"So, either Al-Rousasa is a make-out artist, or he's got some local help," Joe said. "Great. What do we do now?"

"We could go back to the police," Callie said. "That guy just tried to kill you."

"Yeah, but where are the witnesses?" Joe asked.

"What am I? Pizza dough?" Callie said. "I saw the whole thing."

"Yeah, and you just happen to be Frank's girlfriend."

"Joe means we need someone who isn't quite so personally attached to us," Frank tried to explain.

"You mean they'd think . . . they'd say . . ." Callie's face froze in a murderous expression. She jabbed a finger at the radio, and the roar of an old Led Zeppelin number filled the car as she drove back to town.

Joe leaned over to Frank. "I don't think she wants to talk for a while."

Frank nodded absently, trying to figure out what moves they could make.

Warn Walker? But it was obvious that Walker knew of the danger; that was why Fenton Hardy was working so hard. Walker wouldn't pull out of the rally because of a terrorist. It would destroy his whole campaign.

And who else would believe Frank and Joe without proof? Frank could imagine what the FBI would say. "Whatsamatter, kid? Watching too many spy movies?"

"I wonder if we made a call to England . . ." Frank wondered out loud.

"You mean Sir Nigel?" said Joe.

"Bad idea." Frank shook his head. "Did you happen to get his phone number? I don't think he answers casual phone calls. We'd have to work our way up through the bureaucracy. And by the time we did that—"

"Time!" Joe burst out, pounding into the backseat again. "We don't have time!"

"Hey!" Callie switched off the radio. "What are you doing back there? Trying to punch through to my trunk?"

"Sorry, Callie," Joe apologized. "I'm going a little crazy. I don't know what I'm doing." He stared at Frank. "Or what we're going to do."

"*I* know what we're going to do." Frank came

to a decision. "If the cops aren't going to investigate the mall, *we* will."

"Great!" said Callie. "When do we start?"

"Hey, wait a minute," said Joe. "He didn't mean you. He was talking to me."

Callie hit the brakes and pulled to the side of the road. "Well, he meant me, too—unless you want to walk the last couple of miles into town."

"But this is going to be dangerous," Joe said. "And you're a *girl*."

"Gee, it's too bad that guy didn't try to run *you* down, Joe," Callie said. "He'd have wrecked his car on that thick head of yours."

"Callie—" Frank began.

"Are you going to start this 'poor, helpless female' stuff too?" she demanded. "I'll take that from Mr. Macho back there, but not from you. Look," she said, drawing in a shaky breath, "Iola was my friend, too. And I'm going to help. You might as well get used to that."

Frank and Joe looked at each other.

"She's got a point," Frank said.

"Okay," Joe finally agreed. "I just hope you don't regret it," he said to Callie.

"We've got a whole mall to search. Who else do you think should be in on this?" Frank asked.

Joe thought for a moment. "Chet Morton. He deserves the chance."

"And one more person—Tony Prito. He knows the mall, and"—Frank smiled—"there are other reasons. Okay." He turned to Callie. "We meet at your house, one o'clock tomorrow. You call Chet and Tony."

"You're turning me into your secretary now?" Callie asked.

"We don't know who might be listening in on the phone in my house," Frank explained. "And right now you've got an even more important job."

"Yeah?" said Callie. "What's that?"

"Chauffeur," said Frank. "I'd like to get home. I'm beat."

The sun shone brightly on Callie Shaw's yard the next afternoon. But Frank and Joe Hardy moved slowly, their eyes heavy.

"I thought you were going to sleep last night," Callie said, looking at Frank.

"I was. But Joe insisted that we sleep in shifts, keeping an eye out for Assassins." He yawned. "I got eight hours of sleep in two four-hour clumps, with four hours of guard duty in between."

"Well, we're still alive," Joe said, also yawning.

"Yeah," Frank replied. "Barely."

The others who had been called to the meeting arrived together. As they came through the door, Joe found that he couldn't look Chet Morton in the eyes.

Chet stood in silence, running his fingers through his curly brown hair. "Joe," he finally said, his round face serious, "I had a long talk on the phone with Callie last night. She told me a lot of the story. That's why I'm here. If you guys think the killer is in the mall, I want to help."

Joe still didn't look up.

"And I want to say . . . I don't blame you for anything, Joe. Who could expect terrorists in little old Bayport? But we're going to get this guy, right?"

At last, Joe looked at Chet. "Yeah. We're going to get him."

"So what's the plan, Frank?" Tony Prito asked. "Callie said you especially needed me."

"It won't work without you, Tony," Frank said. "We need to search the mall, and we can't do it during shopping hours. We need your help— and Mr. Pizza's. You're the manager, right? Here's what I've got in mind. . . ."

That night, Mr. Pizza was really jumping. Hundreds of kids were hanging out at the mall or heading over to the six-plex movies. And every single one of them seemed to want a slice of pizza.

"Look at that crowd," Callie said to Joe Hardy as she sipped a Diet Coke. "How is Frank going to get past them?"

"We'll see in a second," he answered.

As Frank approached the counter, Tony Prito swung the entrance open for him. Frank stepped into the workspace, right past Chet Morton, who was ordering a slice with the works. Chet didn't even give him a second glance.

"One in. You're next," Joe said.

"Let's give it a couple of minutes," Callie replied. She waited awhile, then worked her way to the fringes of the crowd, aiming for an inconspicuous door off to one side of the restaurants. She leaned against it, hiding one hand with her body, and rapped her knuckles against the cold steel.

Immediately, the door gave way behind her back. Callie slipped in and found Frank standing on the other side. He gave her a quick hug.

"I don't know what it is with you. As soon as you're in a dark place, you get romantic," Callie whispered.

"Romance is wherever you find it," Frank whispered back, looking down the dingy corridor.

Before Callie could answer, another knock came at the door. Chet entered, still eating his slice of pizza.

"Greedy," Callie said. "I thought you'd at least bring some for us."

"Couldn't," Chet said, chewing. "Would have looked suspicious."

"What a detective," Frank commented.

Another knock on the door, and Joe was let in.

"We're all together. Okay, let's go." Frank led the way down the corridor, passing locked doors. "These are the back entrances to all the mall restaurants," he said. "And this one"—he stopped by a door that was ajar—"is Mr. Pizza."

They stepped through the door.

"Charming," Callie remarked, looking around the restaurant storeroom.

"Make yourselves comfortable," Frank said. "We're here until the mall closes."

Time passed slowly in the shadowy room. Gradually the Hardy boys and their friends noticed that less and less noise came from the restaurant outside. They ducked behind a stack of crates as they heard Tony overseeing the cleanup. Then all was quiet.

"Tony's supposed to let people see him leaving," Frank explained quietly. "Then he's got to sneak back in."

Five minutes later, they heard the rattle of keys at the storeroom door. "Hi, guys," said Tony, strolling in. "I just made it back here before they locked everything up. The security guy was getting ready to let the guard dogs loose."

"Guard dogs?" Chet said, turning to Frank. "I hope you thought of them."

"All taken care of," Frank said, lifting a gym bag from a pile of tomato-sauce cans.

"What have you got in there, knockout meatballs?" Tony asked.

"Better than that." Frank pulled a sleek metal pistol from the bag.

"Guns!" Callie exclaimed. "You expect us to shoot?"

*"Dart* guns," Frank explained. "I got the idea from the guys who tried to shoot us the last time we were here." He demonstrated opening the gun, inserting a dart, and snapping the pistol together again. "That will put a dog to sleep for hours—with no ill effects. I had to call in quite a few favors at the zoo and the university to get hold of these, but there's one for each of us."

He passed out the pistols and watched as everyone loaded up. "Here are your flashlights." He smiled tightly. "Well, we're as ready as we'll ever be."

Frank led the others down the corridor. They switched on their lights and opened the metal door. Before them was the food level, the restaurants closed up behind iron gates, the chairs upside down on the tables. The air smelled of old grease and cleaning ammonia. The flashlights barely lit the far walls. The mall was murkily dark and intensely quiet.

"Tony, do you have any idea where those dogs might be?" Frank's voice was hushed in the vast empty space.

"The guy usually lets them loose on the first shopping level. Where they wander after that . . ." Tony shrugged. "It's anybody's guess."

"Upstairs, then. I want to take care of them first."

Tony led the way up a set of service steps. "This is the quickest way. They turn off the elevators and escalators," he explained.

They emerged on the first floor of stores, straining their ears for the clicking of claws on tile, the first hint that the dogs might be in the area.

The stores upstairs were also locked behind metal grilles. "No dogs in there," Joe said, flashing his light into a tie store.

"Guys!" Callie's voice hissed. She'd stepped out onto the circular promenade that overlooked the central well.

Frank and Tony were in the lead as they joined her. "What is it?" Frank asked.

"Look." Callie shined her flashlight on the floor. There lay a muscular, short-haired body—a Doberman pinscher. The dog was on its side, and as they watched its flanks slowly rose and fell.

"Asleep?" Joe whispered, his gun aimed at the Doberman.

Frank knelt next to the animal, gently feeling along its side. He held up his hand, and something glinted in the light.

"Not asleep," he whispered. "Drugged—shot with a dart. Somebody else is in here!"

# Chapter

# 13

"TURN OFF THOSE flashlights!" Frank's voice never rose above a whisper, but it had the force of a cracking whip.

Frank took Callie's hand in the sudden darkness and led her back to the group. "We all move slowly and quietly to the right," he said, his voice barely audible.

They crept to the shelter of a big planter with a potted tree. "I guess he hasn't seen us yet, or *we'd* have been shot with darts," Frank said.

"Do we split up to search?" Joe asked.

"Maybe we should—" Whatever Chet had been about to suggest was cut off by the sound of a store grille rattling up. It came from about a quarter of the way around the circle.

"Builder's Paradise—the hardware store," Joe whispered.

They inched forward until they could see the

beam of a flashlight. A figure stepped from the store, burdened with a bag in each hand and a roll of wire over one shoulder. The flashlight was held awkwardly in the left hand, pointing downward. It gave enough light to show that the figure was male, but it failed to show the face.

Whoever it was turned away from them, heading for the escalator to the lower level.

Joe leaped to his feet. "Al-Rousasa!" he screamed impulsively, aiming his dart gun.

The figure whirled as Joe fired. The dart glittered in the beam of the flashlight but imbedded itself in the roll of wire.

Al-Rousasa didn't waste a second. He dumped the wire on the floor, tossing down a bag and the flashlight as well. The flashlight rolled on the floor, illuminating the search party as they charged along.

The Assassin ducked as Chet fired at him. He rolled behind a planter, digging into his remaining bag. When he popped up from behind the cover, a gun was in his hand.

"Watch out!" Frank yelled.

But even as he did so, Chet gave a choking cry, throwing out his arms. He crumpled to the floor.

Callie fell to her knees beside Chet and dragged him behind a bench, as Frank stood over them, his gun aimed at the planter. Al-Rousasa had ducked down again. Tony crept forward, looking for a shot, while Joe frantically reloaded.

"Chet's unconscious, but still breathing," Callie reported. "He's been hit with a dart."

"A knockout dart for the dogs," Frank said. "We're lucky he wasn't carrying something more lethal." He snagged the bag the Assassin had dropped. Inside were plastic-wrapped blocks of what felt like clay—clay with a pungent smell, when he opened one of the packs.

"What is that stuff?" Callie asked.

"Plastique," Frank replied. "Plastic explosive." He raised his voice, calling to Al-Rousasa. "We know why you're here. And we know that you only have a dart gun. We outnumber you, so why don't you just give up?"

Tony Prito had reached a place where he could both cover the escalator and get a shot behind the planter. "He's not there!" he shouted. "He got away!"

Frank threw down the bag of plastique. "Fan out!" he yelled. "We've got to catch this guy."

"What about Chet?" Callie said.

"He'll be out for the next couple of hours. We'll have to leave him." Frank stepped forward in a crouch, his gun drawn.

"We'd have seen if he decided to walk down the escalator." Joe stood beside his brother, his gun reloaded.

"And we'd have heard if he pulled another of those grille things up," Tony said.

"He's probably lying very still, just hoping

we'll miss him in the dark," said Callie as she caught up with them.

"Okay." Frank gestured the others to gather around him. "We spread out," he said quietly. "No lights, no talking unless it's absolutely necessary. Let's go."

Their skirmish line moved forward quickly but quietly, scanning shadows, peeking around possible hiding places. But there was no trace of Al-Rousasa.

"He can't have disappeared," Joe muttered. "Where is the guy?"

Rattling noises ahead gave them the answer.

"He's raising the grille at Lacey's!" Joe exclaimed in an urgent whisper. He sprinted forward.

"Boy, is the security director gonna be in trouble," said Tony, following. "This guy has keys to all the stores."

Al-Rousasa had raised the gate only a few inches and was scooting under it. They could see his legs disappearing as they arrived.

"He's pulling it down!" hissed Callie.

Joe turned his run into a dive, sliding along the polished tile floor. He jammed his flashlight under the gate just as it slammed down. The grille bounced up, failing to lock.

Al-Rousasa disappeared into the darkness again.

Frank stormed over to his brother. "You made yourself a perfect target, lying on the floor like that," he said to Joe. "If he had stayed two more seconds, he could have put a dart right in you."

"At least we're not locked out," Joe shouted back.

"Yeah, but this is bad," said Tony. "Lacey's has its own escalators and service stairs. It even has separate exits."

"And about a million more places to hide than that walkway out there," Callie said.

"He headed down this aisle," said Joe. "Come on."

It was the main cosmetics aisle, and the Hardys and their friends could smell the various perfumes as they moved forward.

They were just passing the Makeover Bar when a crash from the left caused everyone to swivel around. Then they heard Tony Prito cursing and thrashing in the darkness. "Who moved that stupid chair out into the middle—"

"Three guesses," said Joe, moving ahead faster.

Al-Rousasa popped up from behind the bar to send a dart whizzing toward him. Joe dropped down, and the dart smashed into a display case behind him.

Before Frank or Callie could get off a shot, the Assassin vaulted over the counter and ran down another aisle.

Tony untangled himself and charged after him, only to run into another stool.

"This guy is good," Joe whispered as they set off down the aisle.

"Shhh," said Frank, listening hard for footsteps.

Ahead of them, a glass bottle smashed to the floor, knocked over by Al-Rousasa's elbow. They rushed toward the noise.

But Al-Rousasa was still ahead.

They had reached ladies' hats when Joe suddenly stopped, waved the others back, and grabbed a mannequin head from a counter. He poked the head around the corner, and was rewarded with the hiss of a dart. The plastic head rolled down the aisle with a dart in its right eye. "Heard him reloading," Joe explained as he ran in pursuit.

He was well ahead of the others when a figure popped out of a rack of clothing, tossing a sweater into Joe's face.

Tony fired and missed.

"We'll have to split up to find him," Frank said.

They were like hunters beating their way through a forest—a forest of Orlon, Dacron, and wool.

Callie and Frank met at the end of one aisle. "It's weird," said Callie. "I've been in this store a million times. Now everything seems spooky."

"That's because we don't know—" From the corner of his eye, Frank caught movement. "Down!"

One of the trio of mannequins on a platform had whirled around, drawing a bead on them. As a dart flitted over their heads, Frank and Callie crashed to the floor together, their guns going off.

Neither shot hit Al-Rousasa. The "mannequin" had disappeared.

"Over here!" Frank yelled.

The quick slap of footsteps indicated that Joe and Tony were coming on the run.

"Oh no you don't!" they suddenly heard Joe yell. Then they heard the hiss of a dart.

Frank, Callie, and Tony changed course.

"Caught him trying to sneak down the escalator to the next floor," Joe said.

From the distance came sounds of footsteps on metal treads.

"So he went upstairs instead." Frank ran for the other escalator, only to throw himself flat as something came flying at him.

"I think he's discovered the cutlery department," Tony whispered.

"We've got to get upstairs," Frank said.

"Well, he can't be guarding every way up," Callie pointed out. "You and Joe keep him here. I'll go up the other escalator."

"And I know a set of service stairs," Tony added.

"How do you know about Lacey's service stairs?" Frank asked.

"I, uh, kind of had a thing going with one of the salesgirls in ladies' underwear."

"I'm not going to touch that line," Joe said.

"Get going," whispered Frank.

While Callie and Tony set up the flank attack, Frank and Joe tried to keep Al-Rousasa's attention. They made lots of noise and fired a dart up the escalator. Joe even threw the knife back upstairs. No response.

"Frank? Joe?" Callie's voice floated down from upstairs. "There's nobody here."

"Then where'd he go now?" Joe asked.

A muffled shout gave him the answer.

"Oh, no!" Callie said. "Tony!"

They found the unlocked door to the service stairs—and Tony painfully crawling out of it.

"What happened?" Frank asked.

"Turns out he knew about these stairs, too," Tony said. "He was coming down."

"You met him?" said Callie.

"Met him?" Tony groaned. "I think I've got one of his footprints on my chest!"

"You're lucky he didn't kill you," said Joe.

"Nah. He just knocked me down a flight of stairs and stole my flashlight." Tony started a shaky effort at standing up.

"Take it easy," Callie advised.

"No way. If he took this route, I think I know where he's heading." Tony got to his feet. "I really want to get him now. He hurt my pride." He groaned again. "As well as my chest. Come on."

He led the way down the service steps. "When

we saw this guy first, he was out in the mall. Now he's in Lacey's."

"Isn't Lacey's part of the mall?" Callie asked as they raced down the stairs.

"Yeah, but it's pretty much cut off. Once they get you in this store, the idea is to keep you there. Even the maintenance passageways don't hook up. Except . . ."

"Except where?" said Frank.

"There's a connecting doorway in the third sub-basement. I used it on break time to see Debbie." Tony stopped for a second. "I mean, my friend."

"You've got to hand it to this Al-Rousasa guy," Joe said. "He knows all the make-out spots in town."

"Uh-uh," said Tony. "I think only Debbie and I know about this combination—the door *and* the service stairs. The only other person who might know is somebody who spends a lot of time in the third sub-basement. And I don't think anybody works down there."

"So you're saying it must be Al-Rousasa's hangout," Joe said.

"Or hideout," Frank suggested eagerly. "Where are we now?" He pushed ahead.

"First sub-basement," Tony said.

Frank swung around the landing, then suddenly halted. "I think you may be right," he said quietly, waving the others back. Kneeling down, he shined his flashlight just above the steps.

Callie, Joe, and Tony stared at the thin black line revealed in the light.

"What is it?" Callie asked.

"A trip wire. I caught it just in time," Frank said as he examined it. "Somebody drilled a little eyebolt into the wall here and stretched the wire across to the banister. Want to guess who?" He shrugged. "Still, it could have been worse."

"How's that?" Tony looked puzzled.

Frank's face was serious. "I thought the wire might be attached to something."

"Like a bomb, you mean?" Joe said.

Frank nodded. "But all it's set to do is send you down the next flight of stairs on your face."

Callie shuddered. "Nice guy."

"It means we'll have to be more careful as we head toward that basement. This guy isn't just a fanatic. He's cunning, too cunning for our health."

They found one more trap after reaching the third sub-basement—a deadfall in a corridor, rigged to drop concrete blocks on anyone who tripped it.

"Looks like we're getting closer," Joe said, stepping carefully over the trip wire.

Callie put a restraining hand on his arm. "What's that ahead?"

Ahead of them, the darkness was no longer absolute. The corridor made a sharp turn, and from beyond that bend came a sickly, pale illumination.

"Somebody's got a light on," Tony whispered. "Maybe we should take a look."

They stole down the length of the corridor, Frank checking for any traps. Joe reached the corner and whipped around it, scanning the new corridor, his gun instinctively following his eyes. "Empty," he finally whispered.

The new corridor was indeed empty, but it was better lit. About halfway down the hall stood an open door. The light streamed from a room beyond.

"Some kind of storeroom, I think," Tony whispered. "Nobody uses it, so that light should not be on."

They cat-footed down the corridor, then bolted through the door, guns out, and froze.

Joe was the first to enter the room. "I don't believe this," he said. "Nobody home." The room was small, walled in dirty gray cement blocks. A heavy concrete support pillar rose up in the middle of the floor. Around its base was a pile of grayish plastic explosive blocks, a lot of electronic equipment, several clips of ammunition—and an Uzi submachine gun.

Joe darted behind the pillar. "Well, he's not hiding here. We really have lost him."

"It's not a waste," Frank said, scooping up some of the plastic bricks. "We've got evidence that someone was here, and these show what he was trying to do. The cops will have to listen to us now."

"Very good work," a voice said from the door-way.

The Hardys and their friends whirled around to see the grim face of Inspector Sam Butler, giving them his two-millimeter smile. He was leaning against the door frame, only his face in the light.

"Well, if it isn't the tough cop himself," Joe said. "What's the matter, Butler? Began having second thoughts about laughing us off? Now we've got proof. It's lucky you came along."

"Not exactly," Butler said, stepping into the light. For the first time, they saw the Uzi in his hand.

"Put your pop-guns down," Butler com-manded. "You came looking for Al-Rousasa. Well, now *he* has found you."

# Chapter

## 14

BUTLER GAVE THEIR astonished faces his almost-smile. "Yes, I am Al-Rousasa."

Tony, Joe, and Callie stared in shock and disbelief. But Frank's eyes narrowed. "So *that's* why you didn't understand when Joe made that crack about 'Kojak.' I wondered about that."

"Yes," said the unmasked terrorist. "I had to look that up. You see," he said, "we didn't have those television programs in my country."

"You were one of the guys who tried to nail us in the movie theater," Joe said. "And I bet you sent that van after us, too."

"That interception cost me two operatives," Al-Rousasa said. "And so did the hijacking."

"That's right." Frank frowned in thought. "The government guy talked to you. He must have mentioned where he was going, so you could guess just which flight he'd be on."

"Exactly," the terrorist replied. "They were going to eliminate him while I went to your house to take care of you. We had the element of surprise, I thought."

His voice grew angry. "It seems I was wrong. *You* went on the plane, and my people were surprised. And now I can't contact my superiors." He stared at Frank. "Are you responsible for that? Or is your gray friend responsible? You shouldn't have started associating with him. It's . . . unhealthy. Look where it brought you and your friends."

"You followed us from the police station and tried to run Frank down on the Shore Road," Callie said. "And because you were a cop, you knew about the Lover's Lane on that turnoff."

"Yes, again." Al-Rousasa nodded. "Being a cop has been very useful. Since I was in charge of security for the candidate's visit, I had all the plans of the mall and plenty of time to explore. I didn't expect to find you on those service steps, though," he said to Tony Prito. "I hope you weren't hurt."

"You're pointing a gun at me and hoping I wasn't hurt!" Tony scowled at the gunman.

"What I don't get," Joe said, "is how you can have such a great record and pull off something like this. You're a cop *and* a terrorist?"

"I am an Assassin," Al-Rousasa said proudly.

"*Samuel Butler* was a cop. But Samuel Butler is dead."

"D-dead?" Callie faltered over the word, staring at the man.

"I liquidated him and took his place." Al-Rousasa gave them his half-smile again. "That was easy. The hard part was finding a policeman with the right record, the right build, the right looks, *and* who was starting a new job. Samuel Butler was the perfect identity for me."

"But people knew Butler," Joe burst out. "There must be pictures of him. How could you—"

"The Assassins are very up-to-date on plastic surgery," Al-Rousasa said. "Beyond the state of the art, you might say."

"Plastic surgery. Well, that explains your stone face," Frank said. "Every time you get any real facial expression, you act as if it hurts. I bet it really *does* hurt."

The terrorist's lips thinned. "You're a very clever young man. Dangerously clever. Thanks to you and your brother, my whole mission has been thrown off."

Al-Rousasa glared at the Hardys. "It was so simple—coordinating a series of attacks in major cities. Then came the order to eliminate Philip Walker."

"Since Butler ran the guard detail at the U.N., you'd be sure to get the security job when Philip Walker came to town," Frank said.

"Yes," replied Al-Rousasa. "But your father interfered, gathering information on the Assassins. So then came orders from the Central Committee to punish Fenton Hardy."

"Orders you followed by setting a bomb in his sons' car," Frank added.

The Assassin nodded. "Then there was a further complication. You didn't set the bomb off. Instead a stupid girl—"

Joe lost his cool and lunged for Al-Rousasa. "You murdering—"

The terrorist neatly sidestepped him, ramming the pistol grip of the Uzi into the side of Joe's head. He fell, stunned, and Al-Rousasa turned the barrel of the gun on the others before they had a chance to move.

Hooking the toe of his shoe under Joe's ribs, Al-Rousasa rolled him in front of Frank and the rest of the group. "Enough complications. Now you will all lie down, before we have another outburst."

The Hardys and their friends spent most of the next hour bound hand and foot, lying on their bellies while the Assassin worked in the room. Craning his neck around, Frank saw Al-Rousasa bring in a ladder, then climb to the top of the pillar, carrying bricks of plastic explosive.

He strolled out of the room, leaving them alone for a while. Frank tried to squirm against his bonds, but the terrorist was obviously an expert in the art of immobilizing people. The wire loops around his wrists were beyond his strength. Frank was as helpless as a baby. He stopped his struggles when the Assassin returned, dragging the still drugged Chet Morton.

"I thought you might be missing your friend," Al-Rousasa said, "so I brought him to join you." He climbed up the ladder again. "Just a few more adjustments, and I'm done."

Several minutes later, he came back down. "Now, the final cleanup." He hauled Frank to his feet, testing the wire that bound his hands.

"A little loose. You've been working on these. That won't do." The Assassin grabbed a roll of heavy duct tape, wrapping it around and around Frank's wrists. "That should take care of it," he said. Frank could hardly feel his fingers.

Al-Rousasa pushed Frank against the pillar, using more wire to tie him to it. "Very nice," he said. "I think your lady friend will be next. At least she won't need taping." Callie was quickly tied into place. Then the terrorist worked through the rest of the group, until they surrounded the pillar. Even the unconscious Chet was in place, sagging against his bonds.

"In case you're wondering, this pillar is right below the spot where they'll set up the podium for Philip Walker," Al-Rousasa explained. "He'll arrive at ten-thirty and start to speak. At exactly eleven o'clock, the plastic explosive I've so artfully arranged at the top of the pillar will detonate—all one hundred pounds of it."

The terrorist's voice sounded almost disappointed as he went on. "Your interference has thrown me considerably off my timetable. I'd hoped to set up some antipersonnel bombs around the mall to add to the excitement. But now I'll have to do without them and spend my time cleaning up the mess you made in Lacey's." He sighed. "As your poet says, the best laid plans . . ."

Joe surged against his bonds, aiming a devastating kick at the Assassin.

But Al-Rousasa saw it coming and twisted aside, deflecting the kick off his hip. He grabbed Joe's chin in his hand, forcing his head back into the rough concrete.

"That was a very foolish thing to do." Al-Rousasa glared down into Joe's eyes, his face for once registering anger. "Don't mistake me for Inspector Butler. I'd have no qualms about slitting your throat."

Then his expression smoothed out again as he stepped back. "But I think I can find it in myself to forgive you. After all, you have so little time left before that bomb turns you all into history."

Al-Rousasa stepped to the door. "You notice I haven't gagged you. That's because no one will hear you down here. But I've decided you'll wait in darkness." He gave them his sadistic half-smile as his hand went to the light switch. "Perhaps you'll find it romantic." He looked at Frank, then at Joe. "Goodbye. Inspector Butler has many things to do before the big day tomorrow."

His hand hit the switch, and the naked bulb went out. The last thing they heard was the sound of the heavy steel door slamming shut behind him.

# Chapter
## 15

AL-ROUSASA HADN'T left them in *complete* darkness, Frank Hardy realized. A faint red glow came from overhead. After a moment he realized what it was. The bomb above them had a digital timer, and the glow came from the numbers as they counted down the time until the bomb exploded.

Time! Frank started to look at his watch, but of course his wrists were securely tied together. He tested his bonds again but found no flexibility at all.

Beside him, Joe strained wildly against the wire around his wrists, grunting in exertion.

Frank turned to him. "Can you loosen that wire?"

"Not a bit," Joe responded. "I think I'm cutting my hands off."

"Anyone else tied a little looser?" Frank asked.

From out of his field of vision came Tony Prito's voice. "That guy tied me so tight my hands have gone to sleep." They heard him struggle some more. "I've tried pulling, and I've tried twisting, and neither is doing a thing." He paused for a second. "And Chet's still in dreamland. I don't think we can hope for any help from him."

"Frank, I—I think I've got a little slack," Callie said. "When he started tying us up, I remembered something you had told me about trying to keep my hands as far apart as possible." Callie grimaced. "It hurt like anything, but I tried to keep the pressure up. What do I do now?"

"Press your wrists as close together as you can. Try to make one of those loops big enough to work your hand free," Frank said.

Callie twisted in her bonds as she strained to get loose.

"Ugh," whispered Joe. "I cut myself that time." He worked against the wires on his wrists some more. "Hmm. I thought bleeding might help—might get my hand slippery. But it's just making things sticky."

Frank was still rubbing his sweat-soaked wrists together when he felt Callie resting her face against his shoulder. Her brown hair tickled the side of his face, but she didn't say anything. Then he felt the first spot of wetness hit his shirt. She was trying hard to hide it, but she was crying.

"C'mon, Callie," Frank whispered. "You've got to keep trying. You're our best shot."

"I've rubbed my wrists raw, and it's no good." Her voice broke. "I was wrong, Frank. I can't get loose."

"Callie, you can," Frank said quietly. "Now, give it another shot."

He could feel her blinking the tears away. "Okay."

"Relax. Just let your hands hang there for a second." Frank could feel her shoulder loosen up.

"Good. Press your wrists together. Don't bunch them up." Frank felt her move beside him.

"Now, keep your right hand limp, and see if you can move one of those wire loops down. Come on," he breathed into her ear. "Just slow and easy."

Callie's breath came in little sobs of effort. "Frank? Frank? I think I felt something slip!"

"Guys," said Frank, "I want you to give Callie as much slack as possible. Lean in toward her. Tony? Can you keep Chet from lolling over on her?"

"Okay," Tony said. "Come here, Chet, old man."

"I—I've got one of the loops," Callie said breathlessly. "It's coming down, it's coming . . . it's off!"

"Way to go, Callie!" said Tony.

"I don't believe it," said Joe, mortified. "All us

guys working our tails off to get loose, and we've got to depend on a *girl* to get us out of this mess!"

Callie laughed shakily. "Hey, you should be glad you agreed to let me come along!"

"That's right, Joe," Frank said with a grin. "Watch how you talk to Callie. She may just decide to leave you here." He turned to Callie. "Ready for the next one?"

Even though she'd loosened one loop, Callie still had a long struggle against Al-Rousasa's expert knot job. No one was sure how long it took, but by the time she was almost done, Chet Morton had come groggily back to life. At last, after a couple of setbacks, Callie finally pulled one shaking hand free.

The job went much faster after that. Soon Callie had freed her other hand and frantically loosened the bonds that held her to the pillar. She staggered away, rubbing her wrists, then turned to Frank. She tore at the tape on his wrists. It didn't give. "I can't get to your hands," she said, her voice going high.

"There's a Swiss army knife in my pocket," Frank said. "Use that."

She dug out the knife and began slicing and sawing at his bonds. Soon he was free, too. "Anybody else have a knife?" he asked.

Callie was already at work on Joe. Frank got a pocket knife from Chet and set him and Tony free.

"Great!" exclaimed Joe softly, rubbing his

wrists. "Now let's get out of here and over to Chief Collig. When he sees this setup, he'll hang Butler's hide out to dry."

Joe rushed to the door, grabbed the handle . . . and swore. "I'm getting tired of this," he said, twisting the knob with both hands. He turned around. "Guys, you're not gonna believe it. He locked the door."

"Find the light," Frank ordered. Joe fumbled around until he hit the switch. His brother examined the lock. Frank's face was grim as he looked up. "Tony, what did they expect to store in here? Bars of gold? This door is built more solidly than some vaults I've seen."

"Can't you take the lock apart from the inside?" Callie asked.

"Oh, sure," Frank said. "All I'd need is a cold chisel, or maybe a power drill to ream out these bolts. All we've got is a Swiss army knife." He glanced upward. "Of course, there will be a big hole in the ceiling in a few hours."

They all stared up at the bomb. "He didn't even leave the ladder in here."

"It's getting late now," Chet pointed out. "Our folks will start missing us. Maybe people will come looking."

"Sure," Joe snorted. "And the first place they'll look is the third subbasement of the mall—after hours."

"Maybe it wasn't such a good idea, keeping this search a secret," Callie said quietly. "My folks won't suspect anything till morning, when they find the pillows I stuck under my bed covers."

"There's got to be a way out of this," Joe said, stalking back and forth. "If only we could knock that door down."

"Actually, there is a way." Frank stared at the top of the pillar. "We could blow the door down."

The others followed his gaze to the bomb. "Use *that?*" Chet said. "How will we get to it? What if it goes off?"

"We'll have to form a human pyramid." Frank's eyes were still on the bomb. "And if it goes off, well, it just happens a little earlier."

"Okay," said Joe. "Chet and I will be the bottom, Tony and Callie the middle, and my brother the electronics genius will be the top. Come on."

He and Chet bent over, leaning against the pillar. Tony and Callie stepped on their shoulders.

"Oooohhh," said Chet as he felt Callie's weight. "I don't know what they put in those darts, but the aftereffects—"

"I don't want to hear about them until Frank is done," Joe snapped.

Callie and Tony were in position, and Joe climbed onto their shoulders. He carried his trusty knife, a couple of pieces of wire, and the roll of duct tape.

"Is that enough to do the job?" Callie asked.

"I hope so," Frank answered. "It's all we've got."

Frank tried not to look at the numbers flickering away as he examined the timer.

"Come on," came a gasping entreaty from the bottom of the pyramid. "Pull the thing loose."

"It's not that simple," Frank said, frowning as he began to trace wires. "These things are booby-trapped to keep people from tampering with them."

"*Now* he tells us," Chet groaned.

"Frank can handle it," Joe answered. "Otherwise, it's just sooner instead of later."

"Sneaky," Frank muttered. "Lots of circuits going to the plastique. Some real, some dummies. Some with the detonators hidden." He removed the timer housing, forcing his fingers to keep steady as he probed the innards of the machine. "Yow! Look at all these connections." He extended his knife blade to pry at some wires when the pyramid shifted beneath his feet. He snatched the knife away.

"How's it going?" Joe called up.

"Like brain surgery on a trampoline, except that the medical risk is *ours*." Frank looked down. "Rest time."

It soon turned into a routine—a few terrifying seconds as Frank disconnected circuit after circuit, followed by ever longer rest periods, while pyramid members flopped on the floor.

"Almost there," Frank said during the ninth

rest period. "I've taken out all but three circuits. They're connected to detonators in the plastic explosive. If I can dig them out, that plastique can stay up there forever. But they're tricky . . ."

"Oh, great," Chet muttered. His face was a mild green, with big droplets of sweat standing out.

"Hey," Frank said. "I haven't blown us up yet."

*"Yet,"* Chet repeated.

"I've got to get these circuits all in one go," Frank said. "And I need to have everything as steady as possible. Understand?"

They formed the pyramid again, and Frank climbed to the top. He'd gained a new tool, one of Callie's plastic barrettes for digging through the plastique. It wasn't safe to push metal in there. He scraped into the stuff like a kid playing with Silly Putty. Hidden in the explosive clay were three final circuits—buried detonators. If he could find them, they had a fighting chance.

Frank cleared a wire. He traced it through the plastique to a walnut-sized lump—the detonator. Working very carefully, he dug out the second cap, leaving it surrounded by a small wad of explosive. The exposed charge dangled from the timer box at chest level, sure to kill him if it went off. Frank pushed the thought from his mind and scratched away to find the next connection.

"One to go," he breathed. But dig as he would, he couldn't find a wire.

"Come on . . ." At last, a wire! But where was the detonator? He traced the wire as far as he dared lean, and it didn't end. "We'll have to set up around the other side of the pillar," he said.

It wasn't easy to reassemble the pyramid without resting first, but Frank was insistent. "We can't wait for this. I'm not sure about all these circuits." Frank climbed into the new position, digging away. There was the detonator, halfway around the pillar. With delicate moves, he worked to isolate it.

Below him, Chet Morton began to moan.

"Chet?" Joe turned to his partner in the pyramid.

Chet was gasping, and his shoulders trembled. "I wasn't kidding about aftereffects," he managed to choke out. "I think I'm going to . . ." His hands slid against the surface of the pillar, and the whole pyramid swayed sickeningly.

At the top, Frank lurched, clutched, and pulled the wire free. An insistent beeping started inside the timer.

"Callie! Get a foot onto my shoulder! Tony, shift over!" Joe commanded, grunting as he took the extra weight. Chet, ashen-faced, was able to bear up under the reduced load.

"Frank, what's going on up there?" Joe wheezed, leaning his head into the pillar.

"Tamper alarm." Frank Hardy stared in horror. "It's gonna blow." He reached out as far as he could, grabbed the wire, and pulled. The timer ripped free. "Everybody down!"

The pyramid disintegrated beneath him.

Frank landed on his feet, sprinting to the door. "Get behind the pillar! Hands over ears!" Was it his imagination, or were the beeps growing louder? He slapped the explosive-coated detonators around the doorknob. Was it enough plastique? Or too much?

"How much time?" Joe asked, peering around the pillar.

Frank was already running back. "None."

Behind him, the door erupted!

# Chapter

## 16

FRANK HARDY STARED fuzzily around him. The blast had sent him flying onto the sprawled bodies of his friends. They lay on the floor, coughing from the dust and smoke, looking like a bunch of coal miners. He pulled himself up to examine the door. Had the plan worked?

His heart almost stopped when he saw the door still standing. Then he saw the smoking holes around the doorknob.

The bolt in the lock still held the section with the doorknob in place. But the door itself had been blown loose by the plastique. All they had to do was pull on it.

"Ouch!" Frank croaked, yanking his fingers away. "It's hot!"

Using a piece of torn jacket to protect his hands, Frank pulled the door free. "Now! Up!" he said.

They rushed up the stairs, then onto the Food Floor. The cavernous black pit they'd crossed the night before was flooded with light, packed with people, and full of noise. The rally had started!

"How will we ever get through?" Callie said.

"I'll show you," Joe said, ramming his way into the crowd.

Some people gave them angry looks as the Hardys and their friends shoved them aside. Many more gave way nervously at the sight of five dirty, tired-looking kids in rumpled clothes.

At last they reached the police barricades and climbed right over. "Hey, you little punks!" Officer Con Riley froze in surprise. "Joe? Frank?"

"Let us pass, Con," Joe said, darting around him. "This is an urgent message."

He turned to the podium and stared. It was empty.

Then a lane opened in the crowd on the opposite side of the floor. People began chanting "WALK-ER, WALK-ER!"

"Looks like the candidate was delayed," Frank said.

Waving from the middle of a police escort was Philip Walker, accompanied by Fenton Hardy. And hustling them along, with frequent worried glances at his watch, was Al-Rousasa, alias Inspector S. Butler.

"STOP THAT MAN!" Joe yelled, pointing at Butler. He, Frank, and the others rushed around the podium.

Butler stared at the charging kids with an expression of complete shock on his face. He whirled to face Philip Walker—and found Fenton Hardy standing in his way.

Joe almost reached him, but the terrorist dived through his own astonished police escort and disappeared into the crowd. The surprised cops tackled the kids, wrestling them to the floor. The crowd began to scream as they watched what seemed to be a terrorist attack.

But over all the noise came the furious voice of Fenton Hardy. "Frank! Joe! Why are you here?" His eyes widened as he took in their condition. "And what are you doing?"

Joe tore loose from the policeman who was sitting on him and pointed into the crowd. "Watch out for Butler."

"The cop?" Fenton Hardy asked.

"He's no cop," Frank shouted. "He's an Assassin!"

Fenton Hardy's lean face tightened as he realized what Frank had said. "You're saying he's one of the Assassins? Where did you learn about them? And why are you still in Bayport?"

"We stayed to investigate Iola's murder, Dad. Butler is the one who did it, except he's really called Al-Rousasa, and he's got a hundred pounds of plastic explosive set under that podium."

Fenton Hardy looked more appalled than

shocked. "The Bullet!" he exclaimed. Immediately, he called Con Riley over. "I want half of this detail to stick to the candidate like glue. The other half is to come with us."

"Hardy! What's going on here?" Philip Walker's deep, penetrating voice went perfectly with his appearance. His long dark hair, with just a trace of silver in it, was brushed straight back, and his square chin showed a deep cleft. He was the perfect Hollywood casting for a senator—and maybe for president.

At that moment, though, his famous smile was turned off. "Who are these people?" He glared at Frank and Joe as they were introduced to him. "Your sons! I thought they were coming out to kill me!"

"Someone else is trying to do that," Frank said. "Come with us and see."

Down in the subbasement, Walker's face went as gray as the plastique when he saw the bomb at the top of the pillar.

"The police bomb squad will be here any minute to remove this," Fenton Hardy said. "They're also putting out an all-points bulletin for Butler."

The politician was still shaken. "The man in charge of police security was trying to kill me? It's hard to believe." He looked at Frank and Joe. "I owe you boys an apology."

"Under the circumstances, I'd say it's best to

cancel the rally," Fenton Hardy went on. "At least we won't have to evacuate all those people."

"Cancel?" Walker looked up. "We can't do that."

Fenton Hardy stared at him. "Sir, you've nearly been assassinated. Don't you see—"

"No, *you* don't see. If I don't go through with the rally, it will be political suicide. People will only see me running away from terrorists." Walker shook his head. "I've got to make this speech."

"If you do go through with the rally, it may be *physical* suicide," Frank said. "This guy is really dangerous. He nearly got you once. He nearly got *us*. The safest place for you is out of here."

"But the police are looking for him," Walker protested.

"They haven't *found* him yet," Fenton Hardy pointed out. "For all we know, he could still be in the mall."

"More likely, he's running for his life," Walker said, sounding as if he were convincing himself. He turned to the police escort. "Gentlemen, shall we head back upstairs?"

Fenton Hardy stared open-mouthed at the retreating back of the candidate. Then he turned to Frank and Joe. "Boys, you've had the most dealings with this Al-Rousasa. Do you think he's gone?"

"I think he's still here," Frank said. "He likes to finish his programs."

"I hope he's still here," Joe said venomously. "I want him."

"We'll have half the police detail and all the mall security people searching for him—and as many more cops as Chief Collig can send," said Fenton Hardy.

"Have them concentrate on the off-limits areas," Frank suggested. "Service stairs, maintenance corridors, those sort of places. He's studied the plans here thoroughly."

Fenton Hardy's face tightened. "Wonderful. It's a shame Walker isn't an official candidate yet. At least we'd have Secret Service help."

"Well, Dad," said Frank. "You've got us."

"And Callie, Tony, and Chet," Joe added. "We could circulate on the shopping floors, keep an eye out for him."

Fenton Hardy nodded. "Good idea. We'll work in teams. Chet and I will take the first shopping level, Tony and Callie will take the second, and you'll take the top floor." He led the way to the Food Floor and their reinforcements.

Moments later, Frank and Joe stood in the glass-walled elevator, heading up to the third shopping level. Frank stared out the glass at the crowds of shoppers. "How many people do you think are here today?" he asked.

"Thousands," Joe answered.

"And we're supposed to pick one guy out of all of them." Frank's lips tightened. "I don't like the odds."

"Well, Dad said the cops are sealing the place off—nobody gets in, and everybody is checked coming out." Joe drummed his fingers on the elevator rail.

"This guy is *already* in here—and he knows all the good hiding places," Frank said. "It's like playing hide-and-seek, betting on the game with Philip Walker's life. And Butler has the home-team advantage."

"Al-Rousasa," Joe corrected him. He shrugged. "At least the Bullet has missed so far."

"This is the slowest elevator in Bayport," Frank said, abruptly changing the subject. "I wish it would hurry. I want to be doing something."

"You're beginning to sound like me," Joe said, laughing. "I thought you'd be trying to think your way to a solution."

"We're past the thinking stage," Frank said somberly. "I just hope we catch this guy before he gets another chance at Walker."

The elevator finally reached its destination. The glass doors opened, and the Hardys heard the sounds of patriotic music drifting up from the central well.

"Boy, this is a real production," Joe said. "Look at all the stage lights they set up in the roof." Dozens of red, white, and blue spotlights were anchored into the atrium roof of the mall, their cables snaking down to heavy-duty electrical receptacles at the edges of the central well.

"A real show, all right," Frank agreed sourly. "Let's just hope we can avoid fireworks for the ending." He looked out over the people walking along the promenade. "Don't they have anything better to do? How can we check them all out?"

"And what about the people in the stores?" Joe added.

"We better just forget about them," Frank decided. "Let's concentrate on the railing around the well. He'll have to stand there to do anything. You take the left side, I'll take the right, and we'll keep circling."

Joe nodded. "Sounds like the best we can do."

They set off in opposite directions, scanning the crowds, paying special attention to anyone standing by or leaning on the railing overlooking the central well.

Joe discovered no suspicious characters, though he did find that the railing attracted several kinds of people. He counted three women with baby carriages, and an old woman with a shopping cart there, as well as about thirty-nine kids all resting their chins on the railing, their arms draped over it, watching the rally below.

Apparently, Walker was putting on quite a show. Words and sometimes whole phrases of his speech came floating up—things like "I refuse to be intimidated . . ."

Joe smiled. "You tell 'em, Phil, baby," he muttered.

A little later, he heard the phrase "Freedom from Fear." That drew lots of applause.

Some of the people below chanted, "U.S.A., U.S.A., U.S.A."

Joe stopped. If things had happened differently, Iola would probably be down there, leading those chants. She'd been so up for the rally, so excited over the chance to meet Philip Walker in the flesh. Iola . . .

From below came the words, "A brave girl, brutally murdered by terrorists . . ."

Joe spun away from the railing. Already the candidate was finding a way to use her in his speeches. His jaw muscles tightened as he looked across the well, wondering if Frank had heard what Walker was saying.

It took a minute, but Joe spotted his brother moving quickly alongside the railing, conscientiously checking out everyone he came to. Frank obviously wasn't listening to the rally.

Joe turned away, but his eyes were suddenly caught by the sight of a man coming out of Hi's Bargain Clothing Store clear across the floor from him on the other side of the well. It looked as though he'd decided to wear his purchases—a pair of loud plaid pants, a polyester zippered jacket, and a baseball cap. The bill of the cap was pulled down, and the jacket seemed a trifle large.

The man stopped by a trash can outside the

store and stuffed a large bag inside. Joe turned, trying to get a clear look at the face under that cap. It was thin, darkly tanned. He could see a heavy mustache, and it seemed very still—almost masklike.

Frank had already passed the store when the man ambled out. The guy walked to the railing and leaned over, resting both hands on it. Then he reached up, unzipped his jacket, and put his left hand in the jacket pocket, making the side of the jacket stick out, covering from casual observers what was under his arm.

But Joe was at the perfect angle to see what was there—a mini-Uzi in a shoulder rig.

Joe ducked behind one of the towers that had been built for the spotlights, hiding behind the thick electrical cables before Al-Rousasa spotted him.

The terrorist leaned over the railing, staring down into the central well. He kept one hand in his jacket pocket, but the other slipped slowly inside the jacket. Joe's mouth went dry.

Al-Rousasa needed only a couple of seconds to empty the twelve-bullet clip into Philip Walker and the crowd below.

How could Joe cross nearly a hundred feet of thin air in time to stop him?

# Chapter

## 17

JOE HARDY LOOKED around wildly as Al-Rousasa's hand disappeared into the jacket. No one else had noticed anything out of the ordinary. Should he shout a warning? Would anyone even listen to him? The Assassin was pulling the gun loose. It was now or never.

His eye once again ran over the electrical cables that ran up to the roof. Tearing one of the heavy wires free and gripping it tightly, he stepped back, took a running start, and swung over the railing. Behind him, people started screaming and shouting as he took off.

He could feel the wind in his face as the far side of the well zoomed closer. Now I know how Tarzan feels, he thought.

Al-Rousasa, his Uzi half-drawn, noticed Joe just half a second before Joe swooped in for a perfect two-point landing, planting both feet squarely against the terrorist's chest.

The submachine gun clattered to the floor as the Assassin rocketed backward, arms windmilling. Joe let go of the cable. He landed hard, rolling and skidding right to the door of the clothing store.

Joe jumped to his feet, rushing at Al-Rousasa. The terrorist was also rising, pulling something loose from under the cuff of his trousers. A gun? No. Light flashed on the six-inch blade of a combat knife.

One thing was certain: Joe's jungle-man impersonation had attracted everyone's attention—and concentrated it on him and Butler. Security people and cops were converging from all over. Joe noticed Frank running toward him.

In a quick glance, Al-Rousasa took it all in, too. He vaulted over a bench, kicking the occupant aside, and dove for his Uzi. No cops were near. He might still have a chance to fire.

Joe dove, too, trying to intercept the terrorist.

They crashed together, slamming into the floor. Al-Rousasa searched desperately for the gun. Joe went for the terrorist's knife. He already knew where the Uzi was. It was underneath him. He could feel the squat shape of the gun digging into his spine.

The Assassin put all his weight behind the knife, trying to shove it past Joe's resisting arms and into his chest.

Then he realized where the gun must be. "Fool," he said breathlessly, grabbing Joe by the collar and hauling him up. "Always you get in my way." Al-Rousasa's eyes blazed, and his control of the language began to slip. His English had a definite guttural accent, very different from Samuel Butler's careful speech.

Joe twisted around as he was pulled off the gun. He brought his foot up and kicked hard, sending the Uzi skittering under the railing, almost over the edge of the well.

His teeth showing in a silent snarl, Al-Rousasa hurled Joe against the concrete bench.

The impact brought stars to Joe's eyes. He blinked them frantically and cleared his vision just in time to see the terrorist kneeling over him, raising his knife for the kill.

Joe was trapped against the concrete. Twisting free would only open up his back to the blade. He had just one chance—to catch Al-Rousasa's knife hand. Joe threw up his left hand, grabbing.

And he missed.

A line of sheer agony opened in the palm of Joe's left hand as the knife edge sliced through. Joe gritted his teeth against the pain.

Al-Rousasa's eyes gloated at the sight of the blood.

Joe kicked him in the knee.

The terrorist lurched, and the blade faltered. It missed Joe's throat, scoring a line in the tile beside his right ear.

"Hold it!"

Joe heard the voice of a policeman behind him.

Al-Rousasa hardly looked up. He simply thrust his knife upward. Even as the policeman fell, the terrorist was on his feet again, crouching low, reaching back for his gun. He turned to face Joe Hardy head-on as Joe lurched to his knees. And that was perfect. Joe's fist came up in a powerful roundhouse right, ramming straight into Al-Rousasa's face.

The punch knocked the terrorist outward, his body jackknifing back. The safety rail vibrated like a giant gong as the muzzle of the Uzi rammed into it. Al-Rousasa lost his grip on the gun, and it spun out into empty space.

The terrorist made a wild grab for the weapon. Arms flailing, he toppled over, following his gun into the central well.

Blood pounded in Joe's ears as he saw his enemy go flying. But Al-Rousasa had the agility of a cat. He threw himself around in midair, snatching at one of the posts supporting the safety rail. His fall slowed for one precious second—enough time to give him the chance to cling to the very edge of the floor. He grabbed that chance.

Joe stood, glaring down at those white-knuckled hands and the dark eyes burning with hatred. "You killed Iola, you scum," Joe whispered. "You don't deserve to live."

His body shook with emotion, hands knotting

into fists. Blood flowed between the fingers on his slashed left hand, splattering to the floor. His face was a mask of hatred—and Iola's killer was at his mercy. A quick stomp on those hands, a kick into that despised face . . .

Joe raised his foot, brought it back—and then spun away. "No," he said through clenched teeth, "no. Then I'd be no better than you."

He bent over the rail, extending his right hand. "Come on."

"You are a fool, Joe Hardy," said Al-Rousasa with a nasty grin. "I would never show you mercy."

"I know. That's why I'd make a lousy Assassin. Even lousier than you." Joe leaned out farther. "Reach up and take my wrist. I'll get you up."

Slowly, Al-Rousasa relaxed his death-grip and reached for Joe's right wrist. He tightened his clutch as Joe grasped his wrist. Then Joe brought down his left hand to get a double grip. He was bent over almost double, one leg wrapped around a railing post.

Al-Rousasa struck like a viper. He pivoted on the hand that still gripped the floor, tearing loose from Joe's hold. His free hand slapped Joe's left palm, which was still bleeding. The pain from the slash returned in all its fury as Al-Rousasa hung on, squeezing with all his might.

Excruciating pain pounded up Joe's arm, all the worse since it was unexpected. He flinched, unlocking his leg from the post. The terrorist gave a wild laugh as he kicked out, pulling both of them over the railing.

The crowd of spectators gasped as Frank Hardy fought his way through them. Nobody bothered to help Joe. They all stared as if the fight at the railing were taking place on TV. Frank reached the railing just in time to see Joe topple over it.

"Out of my way!" Frank grabbed his brother's belt, then hurled himself backward. Joe came to an abrupt stop, still dangling far over the railing.

But the grisly game of tug-of-war quickly came to an end. Joe's blood-slicked hand gave Al-Rousasa no grip. The terrorist had time for one incoherent yell as he slid into a three-story fall.

Joe, trembling and pale, watched the body hurtle down. He looked as if he were about to be sick. "W—We should have remembered," he managed to say. "Nobody takes an Assassin alive."

"He lived by blood, and he died by it," Frank said. He helped his brother to his feet. "Well, Iola's murderer got what he deserved. How do you feel?"

"It wasn't enough," Joe replied. He turned away.

# Chapter

# 18

FRANK AND JOE Hardy sat in their father's study, relaxing. Frank lay on the leather sofa, his hands clasped behind his neck. Joe rested in the recliner with his feet up. His left arm was in a light sling, an enormous bandage wrapped around his hand. "This thing looks like the hand of King Tut," he complained.

"Is that any way for a hero to talk?" Frank asked. "You personally overcame the dreaded international terrorist who was about to spray the mall with bullets."

"Yeah, and you're the one who stopped him from blowing the mall up." Joe grinned. "I hear the Mall Association is talking about giving us a reward. Then we'll be rich as well as famous!" He had started waving his hands as he talked but suddenly stopped with a grimace.

"Are you okay?" Frank said.

"I just forgot and moved the wrong hand. That's why the doctors have me in this stupid sling. To keep it immobilized."

Frank smiled. "It makes you look very heroic. At least, that's what all those girls said who were kissing you."

Joe grinned back. "Yeah. Maybe I should wear an eye patch, too." He leaned back in his chair. "Well, tomorrow everything will be back to normal. Mom and Aunt Gertrude will come home."

"We should be glad Aunt Gertrude wasn't here." Frank gave his brother an amused look. "If she'd been cross-examining us, we'd never have convinced Dad of our story."

Working together, Frank and Joe had concocted a tale to explain their escape from federal custody and their discovery of Butler's double identity—without mentioning such things as the Network, British Intelligence, and trips to London.

Their father had also told them about his investigation—going underground, trying to get close to the people in the Brixton safe house, and ending with some nasty comments about the British for raiding the place and making him lose the Assassins. Frank and Joe had to hide smiles when they heard that.

"In a couple of days, the papers will find something new to write about, and people will forget all about us," Frank said. "It will be like nothing ever happened."

"Yeah," replied Joe, but his face clouded over. Frank knew what he was thinking about. One thing had happened that they would never forget. And because of it, they'd never see Iola again.

Frank looked at his brother's sad face, wishing he could say something to make him feel better.

The telephone rang.

Frank hopped off the couch and grabbed the receiver. "Hardy residence," he said. His eyes grew big. Then he motioned to Joe to pick up the extension on the table.

The voice that came to their ears was weak but recognizable. "Well, I see you two finished my case—even though I was out of action," the Gray Man said. "Good work."

"Not so good," Frank replied, thinking about the terrible moments in the sub-basement of the mall. "We didn't figure that Butler was Al-Rousasa until he pointed a gun at us."

"But then you defused his bomb and stopped his last-ditch attack," said the Gray Man. "It's a shame you couldn't have captured him. We'd have learned a lot."

"We're lucky he didn't take me along on his fall," Joe said. "If Frank hadn't been around to stop it . . ."

"The newspaper accounts made no mention of, ah, any organizations being involved," the Gray

Man went on.

"What?" said Joe. "You're annoyed because you didn't get any publicity?"

"No, you handled that side of things just right," the government man replied.

"Even our father doesn't know exactly what happened," Frank said. "We managed to convince him it was a lucky investigation that brought us to the mall."

Joe broke in. "So, if you need a helping hand to—"

"Do research for us?" The Gray Man's tone showed that he didn't want to say any more, not on an open phone line. "That's a possibility. I thought you'd have decided that this was enough."

They heard a female voice in the background. "Speaking of enough, sir, you've been on that phone far too long. You have to get your rest."

"My nurse," the Gray Man growled. "It's worse than a prison in here. But there's one more thing I want to say."

"What's that?" asked Frank.

"Thanks, kid. I owe you one for saving me from that bomb. When I'm on my feet again, I'll give you a call. Maybe you can come down to New York for lunch."

Before Frank could say anything, he heard sounds of a scuffle over the transatlantic line. "I must insist, sir," the nurse said.

"Give me that back! If I could use both hands . . ." The Gray Man gave an exasperated snort. "At least let me say goodbye."

Frank and Joe grinned at each other as they made their farewells and hung up the phone. "So," Frank said, "we now have a friend in the government."

Joe's face was serious as he nodded.

"You really meant what you said about doing more business with him, didn't you?" asked Frank.

"This is more than just doing something for Iola," Joe said. "I realized it when that killer was falling." He looked at Frank. "As long as there are Assassins, there'll always be more Al-Rousasas."

Frank stared at him. "So you're going to fight them single-handed?"

"No. Not single-handed," said Joe. "That's why I wanted a line to the government. And we've got that reward money coming. Enough to replace our car and get some good equipment." He paused. "And I hoped you would be in it, too." He gazed at his brother's face, frozen in thought. "Look, it's not like I want us to give up our usual cases. But there are bigger things going on these days and we could make a difference."

"We?" said Frank.

"Sure. I need you. What could I do without the brains of the outfit?"

Frank began to smile. "Probably go around

punching all the wrong heads." He stuck out his hand. "All right. Just you and me—and the bad guys."

Joe grabbed Frank's hand with his good one. "Way to go!"

# Frank and Joe's next case:

Disguised as punk rockers, Frank and Joe infiltrate a gang of gunrunners. But the mission goes disastrously wrong, stranding the Hardys in Paris with no money, no passports—and a charge of murder hanging over their heads.

The only way out is working for Reynard and Company, a cold-blooded corporation that treats murder and terrorism like big business. Can the Hardys stop these corporate killers? Or will the killers stop the Hardys—permanently? Find out in *Evil, Inc.*, Case #2 in The Hardy Boys Casefiles.